THE GATHERING

Book Three in the Gift of Grace Trilogy

Debra Yergen

Whole House Publications
S·E·A·T·T·L·E

Debra Yergen

Dedicated to my mom, who has loved me as herself and
taught me so much through Aunt Harriet's eyes.
Happy Mother's Day, every day.

CONTENTS

PREFACE

On January 17, 2015, I awoke the day after my mom's birthday feeling conflicted. I realized that one day I would not have her, and I would live with regret. I have always loved my mother, but I didn't never doubted her love for me. She is sincere and the ultimate optimist, but we have always struggled to communicate. Loving her was not enough. I needed to find a way to see her through her eyes, understand her, and celebrate our differences.

As a writer, I enjoy getting to know and understand each of my characters from their own eyes as their stories unfold. I enjoy learning their motivations and embracing their uniqueness. And so, in building a story and a family around my Aunt Harriet character, I received the gift of "insight" into my mom as I got to know Harriet.

Harriet has the best intentions. Harriet's heart is always in the right place. Harriet is sincere; she never second-guesses the decisions she makes. I admire Harriet's conviction and self-confidence. I am entertained by Harriet, and I love that most readers name Harriet as their favorite character, and someone who frequently reminds them of their own mom.

Today, my relationship with my mom is solid, positive and a gift I treasure more with each passing year. I love her, I embrace our differences, and I smile when I make the effort to see her through her eyes. We still have our differences and our challenges, but I am forever grateful to Aunt Harriet for helping me better understand my mom. One day, I will lose her, and I know that will trigger feelings of great loss. But having taken this journey with her, I will say goodbye without regret. The *Gift of Grace* trilogy has forever altered my relationship with my mom, and for me, that has been the greatest gift.

PROLOGUE

The Isabelle we meet in Book 1: *The Eulogy*, is at times hard to like. Like so many of us, she is spread too thin. Her marriage is challenged. Her relationship with her brother is complicated by their past. Her relationship with her surrogate mother, Aunt Harriet, is at times tense. She works hard to be the best mother possible to Grace, but that too is strained by her schedule, disorganization, guilt, and buried resentment. Isabelle wants to do better and be better, but her circumstances and the demands on her (many self-inflicted) are destroying her confidence and energy.

The Eulogy is Isabelle's opportunity to jump out of her own head and learn to trust those closest to her. What's driving her bickering with her brother? Does her marriage still have a chance? Will she be able to patch up her relationship with Aunt Harriet in time, and will she make peace with herself?

In Book 2: *The Bench*, Isabelle is grieving. She's juggling motherhood in a world she never imagined. On the outside, she's falling apart; on the inside, she is still connected to her decency and drive to protect all the people in her life she loves. She is searching for answers, and although she doesn't realize it yet, she's growing. A series of angels come into Isabelle's life to reveal the miracles that surround her, and remind her that she's not alone. Isabelle begins to take one leap of faith after another on her journey to become the woman she is destined to be.

Debra Yergen

And so Book 3: *The Gathering,* begins.

ACCEPTANCE ▪ TRANSFORMATION ▪ TRUST

Book 1: *The Eulogy,* begins the voyage with a story about acceptance and the journey to like the ones we love.

Book 2: *The Bench,* deals with transformation and the passage to reclaim the dreams we know are possible.

Book 3: *The Gathering,* brings home the importance of trust and the way we learn, live, and offer generous helpings of forgiveness to ourselves and those who share our path.

Join the conversation at https://www.facebook.com/YergenTrilogy/

CHAPTER 1

Wipeout! Surfing was Isabelle's second favorite way to start the day. Nothing about surfing in West Maui was practical, but Isabelle decided to go for it anyway. Practical didn't naturally register that high on her priority list – unless it was related to a parenting commitment or some other adult obligation she was unable to ignore. It had been years since she picked up a longboard and set out in search of a wave swell. A small voice inside told her it might not be a bad idea to take a refresher lesson, but she quickly dismissed that thought. She remembered enough to get out before eight o'clock so she could be back on shore before the wind kicked up mid-morning.

The lack of good waves made locals extra protective of the unspoken rules. Isabelle wasn't looking for good waves, but rather a few small swells without wind to wet her whistle. She remembered enough to know that being a new face in the lineup never garnered much aloha to unseasoned, drop-in surfers. Her chief concern was to avoid getting in anyone's way.

For practical reasons, she felt it made more sense to just rent a board on-site for an hour rather than going to the effort of hauling it from an off-shore discount rental. Plus, she only had time to get out there once on this trip, to keep a promise she made at her late husband's celebration of life a few years before.

If only she would have rented a board on-site at the Sands of Kahana, she could have saved herself the angst of minding the twisty island rules. Mostly tourists trolled those waters for less adventuresome sports like snorkeling and paddle boarding. To catch a wave at the Sands she had to paddle out a quarter of a mile in water that was occasionally known to host sharks, especially after a storm or heavy rain. In fact, a surfer died from a shark attack back in April of 2004, an event that most tourists had no idea about but that was still fresh in the minds of those who frequented the shore.

Sitting on her board, legs hanging over each side, Isabelle could see in the distance a big wave, the kind surfers wait for, sandwiched between two much smaller waves. She took a deep breath, inhaling both excitement and courage. The clean, clear, warm saltwater healed and nourished her skin and purified her soul. She could spend hours on the water if it weren't for her sunscreen wearing off or her stomach feeling seasick – which had only happened to her once, decades ago, when she was in the water for nearly four hours straight. Those days of reckless abandonment were left in her youth. Isabelle had become more aware of her actions and their consequences over the years.

In her attempt to win friends – or at least avoid making enemies – instead of paddling out for the first or second waves, she held back a bit and paddled out to the peak of the smaller tail wave.

It was a fine attempt, but there wasn't enough swell in the water to give her the power she needed. It was just as well; she knew her skills were no longer advanced enough to handle the big waves. She made a few more attempts, wiping out mostly, but catching what she considered to be one perfect wave. For Isabelle, few things in life compared to the sense of accomplishment she felt in executing a perfect wave. There was nothing to show for it except the pure exhilaration of the ride and knowing she still had it in her.

After drinking more saltwater than she would have liked – and to be fair – a tablespoon was more than she would have liked – she decided to go in for the day. At least now she could return to the mainland knowing she kept her promise. Isabelle was tired and despite her regular workouts, she forgot how exhausting surfing could be.

As she hiked back up the shore incline with the board, she noticed a man with a baseball hat sitting on some rocks taking pictures with a long lens. Normally she wouldn't have paid any attention, but she recognized the Oregon O on his hat, and she couldn't resist talking to a fellow Duck. She set her board on the rack, and walked toward him.

"Go Ducks," Isabelle said to the tan, handsome stranger with dark hair and eyes.

"You always been a goofy foot?" he asked. This caught her off-guard. She stared at him silently and somewhat indignant for a moment before smiling. He impressed her with the fact that he noticed she surfed with her right foot ahead of her left on the board.

"I have a lot of bad habits," she laughed, flirtatiously. "Clearly you know something about surfing. So why are you out here on the rocks and not joining the line-up?"

"Unfortunately, I'm better at grubbing than shredding these days so it's easier to stay behind the lens," he said tipping his head toward his camera.

"I'm from Oregon too, although I've been spending so much time in Washington, I think I see more desert than water these days," Isabelle said.

"I'm Owen. What makes you think I'm from Oregon?" he asked.

"Your hat," she said, with an obvious tone, now questioning his apparel.

He pulled off the green baseball hat, looked squarely at the insignia and nodded. "My godson is going to the University of Oregon. He gave me this, I think to say thanks, when I slipped him some spending money," Owen said.

"Oh," Isabelle said, disappointed.

"What's your name?" Owen asked.

"Isabelle," she said casually, no longer interested in sticking around. "I should go," she said cutting him short.

"I was just going to grab some coffee at Bad Ass. Can I buy you a cup?" he asked.

Isabelle wasn't terribly interested but for lack of an easy way to decline the harmless invitation for something she wanted anyway, she agreed. Isabelle rarely turned down coffee, and never turned down island brew. "I guess I have a few minutes," she said. Inwardly, she reasoned that the moment she got bored she'd simply make the excuse to get back to the condo.

On their walk to the coffee shop, in the parking lot across the street from the strip mall, Isabelle unlocked a red, mid-size rental car and pulled out her purse. She looked at the screen on her iPhone to see two missed calls. "Of course, Aunt Harriet," Isabelle said aloud. "She probably wants me to stop at Star Noodle on the way home."

"Isn't it a little early for udon?" Owen asked.

"The girls love their malasadas. They're a fried pastry with filled centers and..." Isabelle didn't get to finish because Owen enthusiastically cut her off.

"I know what they are. They remind me of the beignets at Café Dumond in New Orleans," Owen said. *Show off.* Isabelle wasn't sure if she liked his know-it-all approach. *He's kinda cocky.* "Have you been there? To Café Dumond?" Owen asked.

"Nope. I'm pretty much a west coast girl," Isabelle said.

Did I really agree to have coffee with this douche bag? Ugh.

By no means did Isabelle plan to lose track of time and still be talking to the professor an hour later. She did come to the conclusion that while he may have known the surfing lingo, that was just about all he knew with regard to the sport. As a scientist, it wasn't completely surprising to her that he was intrigued by the mechanics though. Isabelle always considered surfing a sport that balanced mechanics with skill, and truth be told, she was barely more than a novice herself.

Isabelle wasn't sure why the professor seemed so familiar to her; she only knew he did.

"So you grew up in Ellensburg. What year did you graduate?" Owen asked.

"I was born in Ellensburg. I went to high school in Portland and college in Eugene. It's a boring story. Oh look at those cute mugs on the wall," she said, clumsily trying to change the subject.

Do I know this guy from somewhere? "Are you from Ellensburg?" she asked, reticent that the subject might come back to her formative years, and God forbid, the accident.

Owen looked oddly familiar but she couldn't place him exactly, and although he realized their connection half way into coffee, he didn't reveal it to her.

"Totally boring story," Owen said.

"That's fair. I should get home anyway. The kids will be up and ready for breakfast," she said as an excuse to break away. She knew, in fact, the kids were up, and that Harriet had no doubt already fed them. Just then, her phone buzzed again. It was Harriet. "I need to take this." Isabelle smiled.

Before walking back to her car, Isabelle leaned in to hug the attractive professor. Neither of them noticed that Isabelle's chain with Arnie's wedding band caught on a button on Owen's shirt when she pulled back. He was mesmerized as he watched her walk away. She held no expectation of seeing him again, and she certainly didn't give him her contact information. Owen didn't immediately notice the important chain on the ground, blending into the gravel beside his right foot.

As he turned to step away, a woman walking toward him with groceries in a bright green reusable sack pointed out that he had dropped something. He looked down to see the chain and the wedding band, which he recognized from Isabelle's neck. "Thank you," he told her casually, as he bent down, picked it up and slid it into his pocket. "I need to get the latch fixed."

❖ ❖ ❖

Isabelle walked into the condo at the Sands of Kahana with a bag of fresh, hot malasadas. She specifically requested a side of the Sake Caramel, Harriet's favorite. "Did you get…" Harriet started to ask about the caramel, but got cut off by Isabelle.

"Of course," Isabelle said, pleased with herself.

"Thanks honey," Harriet said. Isabelle's daughters, twelve-year-old Grace and three-year-old Hope, were lounging on the L-shaped sofa watching television. Both were dressed and hair combed and styled. This was definitely one benefit to having Harriet stay with them. Back in Portland, Isabelle was mostly on her own as a single mom since her husband Arnie had passed away. She was, of course, thankful for the intermittent help from her brother and sister-in-law, but most of the daily responsibilities fell squarely on her shoulders.

"You were in the water a long time," Harriet observed.

"The line-up was busy this morning," Isabelle offered. Isabelle debated telling Harriet about Owen, and but decided against it since it would only lead to more questions. And since Isabelle had no plans to see him again, she didn't see the point in talking about him

"I'm going to shower. I'll be right out," Isabelle said as she walked to the bathroom.

Isabelle panicked when she undressed and noticed the chain with Arnie's wedding band was missing. She was so careful with the chain. She touched it numerous times a day – every day – it was her go-to habit when she felt stressed and needed to connect to his presence. She threw a towel around herself and hurried back outside the bathroom to the living room, then the dining room and finally, the kitchen. "I lost my chain. Do you see it? Can you help me find it?" she asked Harriet.

"Did you wear it surfing?" Harriet asked.

She did. Isabelle wanted to curl up in a ball on the floor. She remembered looking at it in the car mirror on the way to Honokowai and thinking she should take it off. Her heart sank. *I lost it in the ocean.* She started to whimper.

"Crying's not going to fix it," Harriet couldn't resist holding back her practical but totally unhelpful advice. "You need to be more careful next time."

"There isn't a next time, Harriet," Isabelle snapped. "There was one Arnie. One ring. I lost the last piece I had of Arnie. I wore it to keep him close to me and I lost my last piece of him. I was so stupid. How could I be so stupid?" Isabelle sat on the floor, exasperated, and naked except for her towel.

"I can't indulge you this way," Harriet said.

"You never indulge me," Isabelle voiced her broad-sweeping observation, feeling equally sorry for herself and angry.

"You haven't been like this in a year. I thought you had your life pulled together. Besides, isn't your last piece of Arnie your daughters?" Harriet asked.

This observation stopped Isabelle from spiraling down her path of pity. *I guess Harriet has a point.* She looked up and saw Grace standing about ten feet away looking at her. "Are you okay, mom?" Grace asked.

After all this time, why do I go here? I'm not this person anymore. "Yes, honey. I lost something very important to me, but things are just things. I have you and Hope and that's what matters."

"And Yia Yia," Grace added.

"Yes, and Yia Yia," Isabelle conceded. Over the years Isabelle had stopped wondering how Grace came up with the nickname Yia Yia for Harriet. She started calling Harriet that as a child and somehow it stuck. Not only that, now that Hope was starting to talk, she too had adopted the nickname. So Yia Yia it was.

"Mom."

"Yes Grace."

"Are you going to get dressed?" It was only in that moment when Isabelle acknowledged she was sitting in the dining room naked, except for the plush beige towel wrapped around her torso. *This is so crazy. How did this become my life?* Isabelle sniffled and then sighed. Nearly four years out from Arnie's death she was still forced to take each day as it came. Most days, she held it together. But the smallest upsets could completely turn her world upside down.

"I'm going to shower and then I will get dressed," Isabelle announced. She couldn't help but still feel devastated by the loss of Arnie's ring.

Harriet looked over at Isabelle without saying a word. While the two women had made peace with their shared past – the past that involved mourning Joy – they still seldom saw eye-to-eye on the daily choices of how to respond to life. It was all Harriet could do to resist stepping in to co-parent Grace and Hope, but a promise was a promise. And it was a promise Isabelle held her to.

Isabelle's eyes squinted in sadness as she walked back to the bathroom to shower. She reached up and scratched her head. Losing Arnie's ring was not something she would be able to let go of easily, but she had no choice than to move forward. The ring was gone. She knew she wasn't going to get any sympathy over it from Harriet. And now with Grace entering Middle School in a few weeks, Isabelle faced the new challenge of up-ending that apple cart as well. If she made too big of a deal about losing Arnie's ring around Grace, she was pretty sure this topic would be thrown back in her face by Grace at the most inopportune time.

Over the past year, Grace had become more sensitive to the slights she felt by her friends and family alike. It was all Isabelle could do to keep up with who she liked and didn't like on a week-by-week basis. Isabelle knew only too well the struggles she faced with Harriet growing up nearly thirty years ago, and she wasn't about to be the same *mean mom* to Grace. Grace wasn't even a teenager yet and Isabelle could already see and feel the early signs of her precious child growing her own wings and pushing Isabelle out of the way as she tried, perhaps prematurely, to fly. Isabelle took a deep breath. *Hang on. No doubt things are about to get bumpy.*

It was the middle of the night when Isabelle was awoken by Grace in the bed next to her in the same room. She was having a nightmare. "Come back. Come back, Yia Yia. You're going to get burned," Isabelle heard the child yell out. Isabelle was out of her own bed and by Grace's side within seconds. Grace was physically pushing her away as Isabelle struggled to calm her daughter's arms. Isabelle was glad that Hope was in the other room with Harriet. Even Isabelle felt scared watching her daughter struggle with this trauma in her dreams this way.

"Honey, you're okay. You're having a bad dream."

"Yia Yia's in the fire," Grace said, still half asleep.

"There's no fire. We're in Hawaii. You're okay. Mama's here," Isabelle held Grace close to her chest. "You were having a bad dream."

By this time Grace was awake. "She ran back into the fire to get the book. I was outside and calling to her to come back, Grace said, recalling her dream.

"Who, Yia Yia?" Isabelle asked.

"Yes, Mom."

"Honey, there's no fire. Yia Yia is in the other room with Hope." Just then Harriet showed up in the doorway.

"Is everything okay?" Harriet asked.

"Yep. Just a bad dream. See honey, Yia Yia is right here. It was just a bad dream. You're okay. We're all okay," Isabelle said as she cradled her growing girl.

Harriet had a distinctively alarming look on her face that revealed concerns she hadn't previously shared with Isabelle. Isabelle noticed this look but didn't mention it. She knew this wasn't the time to further alarm her daughter. Harriet walked away and came back with a glass of water for Grace.

"Thank you," Isabelle said, taking the glass of water from Harriet and handing it to Grace. "Do you want some water?" Grace nodded yes and took a few sips before setting the glass down on the white-washed wicker table.

Isabelle glanced over at the little black alarm clock by the cream-colored lamp. The digital clock on the table read two twenty-two. "Do you want to try to go back to sleep?" Isabelle asked Grace.

"Can I sleep with you?" Grace asked.

"Yes, of course," Isabelle said. This was shocking to Isabelle, who had spent the last two years feeling like her daughter had pushed her away every chance she got.

"I'm heading back to bed," Harriet said. "If you need anything, call."

"Thanks. Good night, Harriet," Isabelle said.

"Good night, Yia Yia," Grace called out.

"See you in the morning," Harriet said.

Isabelle lied awake long after Grace fell back asleep. Isabelle wasn't looking forward to the morning. She hated leaving the islands. If Isabelle could have her way, the whole family would move to Maui forever: Grace, Hope, Harriet, her brother Zach and his wife Amone. She would want Carrie there too. Over the past four years, Zach and Isabelle had come to include Carrie, and even tease her like a sister.

Isabelle was so tired of rainy Portland, and this whole business of spending weekends driving to Ellensburg. All this was intended to help Harriet manage an old yellow house, once owned by Zach and Isabelle's parents. It wasn't Isabelle's ideal way to spend her quote-unquote-downtime.

When Harriet first decided to move back to Ellensburg, to the same house where Zach and Isabelle grew up, Isabelle welcomed the opportunity to feel their mother's presence once again. She remembered exploring every closet of the house, feeling certain there was something important hidden in the attic or a secret hope chest. Of course, time would reveal that there was no hidden closet or long lost chest. Her only discoveries were spider webs and beetles with hard shells and wings that scared the daylights out of Isabelle when they flew at her unexpectedly.

The small, hundred-year-old home with the large yard

and rock fence perimeter was too much for Harriet to manage alone. Luckily, she had Zach, Amone, Isabelle and Carrie to constantly help her deal with the yard and upkeep the roof and other structural needs the lot entailed. With winter coming, Isabelle was ready to unload the house and convince Harriet to return to a lovely retirement center in Portland. Of course that was a long shot as Harriet had no intention of leaving the house her sister once owned. But this was Zach's plan, and by extension Isabelle's plan, at least for the time being.

This is what Isabelle pondered for the hour or so before she fell back asleep her last night in Maui.

The next morning, Harriet was up early packing for their flights. Little Hope was still snuggled in Harriet's bed when Isabelle got up. Hope was such a good little sleeper for a three-year-old. Isabelle hoped this was healthy but figured she'd give her a few months before she became too alarmed by the child's penchant for extended naps and late mornings in bed. Isabelle was admittedly overwhelmed and she was at least able to admit to herself how much she appreciated the reprieve from managing a normally high-strung toddler.

Hope was so different from Grace. Grace was inquisitive and practical from the time she was Hope's age. Grace asked a hundred questions about everything at that age, and then several follow-up questions for every answer Isabelle gave. She was simultaneously magnificent and utterly exhausting. Hope was calm and effortless by comparison. And now with Grace being pre-adolescent, Hope's easygoing nature was even more appreciated by her mom. Isabelle wasn't sure she could handle two children like Grace at the same time.

With the two girls outside of earshot Isabelle cornered Harriet. "What was the strange look on your face last night when Grace talked about her dream? Why was that?" Isabelle asked pointedly.

"Honey, I don't know what you mean," Harriet said.

"I believe you know what I'm talking about." Isabelle persisted.

"I heard her screaming. I came in. I got water. I don't know what look you're referring to," Harriet said.

I don't believe you.

"You don't have to believe me. I heard her cries and went to check on you both to make sure you were okay. Beyond that, I don't know what you're looking for." Harriet said.

Isabelle believed that Harriet knew more than she was letting on. It was written on her face. But she couldn't really press her aunt as she genuinely had no idea what she was looking to learn. She just knew something didn't make sense. With a flight in four hours, and an hour drive into Kahului, and four people who still needed breakfast, this wasn't the time to push it. But this conversation wasn't over. Isabelle would revisit the topic when the time was right.

After she finished packing, Isabelle created a hodge-podge breakfast buffet of leftover ingredients. Cereal, eggs, toast, sausage, yogurt. There wasn't enough of any one item to feed everyone the same thing, but there was more than enough leftovers from the week to adequately feed the group a little of this and a little of that. She poured the end of the orange juice for the girls and made coffee for Harriet and herself.

Harriet and Isabelle made a final sweep of the condo before they loaded the luggage and girls into the car for the drive to the airport. They stopped at the front desk to turn in their keys and say goodbye to Gremmie, the long-time resort manager. "Good bye Sands of Kahana," Isabelle said.

"Until next year," Harriet added. Isabelle hoped there would be a next year at the Sands. So much had happened here with their family over the years. It was always home away from home, no matter where home was at the time.

Isabelle tried to focus as she drove the winding road back to Kahului. The majestic blue water on her right both calmed her spirit and called her to stay. She didn't want to leave the trade winds. She didn't want to leave Arnie yet again. It had been three years since she had release his ashes to the sea; driving away felt like leaving him all over. And now, she left his ring as well, no doubt tumbling in the same waves, she believed. She couldn't think of that now. They had a plane to catch and she couldn't think about any of this now. But she would think about it again. She couldn't help it.

CHAPTER 2

Back home in Portland, Isabelle scurried about trying to get Grace ready for her brother, Zach, to pick up for the weekend. Zach and his wife entertained their nieces in exchange for Isabelle agreeing to check on Harriet in Ellensburg. Sometimes, those visits took place monthly and other times weekly. On this weekend, Zach and Amone offered to watch Grace while Isabelle prepared her road trip with Hope.

"You packed your toothbrush and floss, right?" Isabelle asked, emphasizing the conjunction because Grace didn't enjoy flossing any more than most kids do.

"Oh Mother, yes," Grace begrudgingly responded.

"Do you have a jacket?" Isabelle asked Grace.

"Stop treating me like I'm a dumb baby," Grace insisted.

"Do you have your cell phone charger?" Isabelle questioned.

"You're the one going to the dark ages. Not me. I'll be ten minutes away if I forget something," Grace pointed out. *I guess she's right.*

Isabelle had packed a bag for herself and three bags for Hope. Looking at the pile of belongings ready to load into the car made her laugh. *Since when did I become the light packer? Since I became a mom and my life revolved around my kids – that's when.*

The doorbell rang.

"Come in," Isabelle shouted from the other room. "Oh hi," Isabelle said, surprised to see Amone instead of her brother.

"Zach took Winnie to the vet this morning for her shots and there was an emergency ahead of him so he texted me to pick up Grace," Amone explained.

"I'm glad it wasn't Winnie with the emergency," Isabelle said.

The last time a family pet had an emergency, it was Isabelle's dog Snoopy that was badly injured; that event set off a chain reaction that changed the trajectory of Isabelle's life. Every time Isabelle thought about that day, she couldn't help but pause and look up. Indoors or out, she could never forget the moment that commenced her journey to faith in something bigger than herself. Even though she had grown calmer and more even-tempered, life still threw challenges at her, and on occasion she still took the bait.

Today she fought it. Agitation was clawing at her back as she felt the pressure of wanting to get on the road. Instead of letting it win, she took a brief moment to reflect, barely a pause, a few seconds at most, and then continued getting ready for her trip.

Isabelle called into the other room. "Grace, Aunt Amone's here. Are you ready?" Turning to Amone she continued, "We have some attitude going this morning." Isabelle smiled in exasperation. "And she's not even a teenager yet."

"It's all good," Amone said.

"We'll see if you feel the same way by tomorrow night," Isabelle said, just as Grace walked into the room.

"Are you telling her how terrible I am? I'm so so terrible, Aunt Amone. Just ask her." Grace sarcastically added. "I'm ready. Is she ready? I bet not," Grace poked at her mom.

"Watch it, young lady," Isabelle reprimanded her daughter.

"We're going to have fun." Amone broke the tension with a promise to separate her niece and Isabelle.

"Thanks," Isabelle said to Amone. "Grace..." Isabelle spoke her daughter's name and then paused.

"What?"

"I love you. Be good for Zach and Amone."

"I'm always good," Grace said.

"Grace?" Isabelle did not appreciate her daughter's attitude.

Grace finally conceded. "I will. I love you too," the young girl begrudgingly wrapped her arms around her mom to say goodbye.

"You sure you don't want us to take both girls?" Amone asked.

"Nah, we're good," Isabelle affirmed. Isabelle watched Amone and Grace walk down the sidewalk before she made the final trips with the bags for herself and Hope to the car in the garage. She grabbed a sippy cup for Hope and filled it a third full with ice and water and a splash of apple juice on the top for flavor. "Here we go, baby girl," Isabelle said as she picked the toddler up and belted Hope into her car-seat.

She debated handing Hope the cup of liquid, knowing the little girl would likely fall asleep within five minutes of the car pulling out of the garage. Isabelle decided to keep the cup in the front seat with her. If she needed to pull over to give it to her, she could.

Isabelle had made enough trips to the small town in Washington at this point that she no longer needed to type the address into her GPS system. These visits were more Zach's idea than hers anyway, and if it hadn't been for Grace's developing attitude and strong will, Isabelle might have told her brother that he needed to make the trips to Ellensburg himself to check on their aunt.

But the two-day reprieve from Grace seemed to be a fair trade so Isabelle happily went along with her brother's requests to check on their aunt and report back.

Out of the blue, earlier in the week, Harriet had expressed new ideas for additional construction on the Ellensburg home, prompting Zach and Isabelle to step in to assist her without delay. When Harriet first mentioned the updates she planned for the house, not long after Arnie's celebration of life, Zach and Isabelle didn't give much thought to what their aunt planned. If anything, they thought it might give her something to focus on as she continued to recover from her stroke.

Everything changed when the bills started rolling in – bills that made their way to Zach as her power of attorney and concerned money manager. Harriet had commenced quite a few updates to her house and the surrounding property before the kids paid close attention to the construction site. That was all about to change.

Harriet had more than enough money to make whatever changes she wanted to the little yellow house. Her ability to pay the bills was never in question. What was in question from Zach's perspective, was *why* she was sinking so much money into a lot that would never return her investment in terms of market value when it was time to sell. But Zach never involved himself directly in these discussions. Instead, he planted a bug in his sister's ear and encouraged Isabelle to argue it out with Harriet.

This three-year project was on the verge of getting out of hand, and Zach was counting on his sister to talk good sense into their aunt. What started out as minor landscaping updates morphed into a complete redesign worthy of a small estate. The once modest yard with the rock wall that Zach and Isabelle's dad had built was now transformed beyond what anyone – except apparently Harriet – imagined. The yard now included a prominent rock wall perimeter with cast iron gates, and a large yard meticulously sculptured with water features and bronze statues. It was an extravagant adornment for the modest yellow house that prior to the updates hadn't been worth more than about one hundred and fifty thousand dollars.

Just this week, Harriet expanded her vision to include a year-round atrium, which she wanted to have built out the back of the house, to bring the feeling of the outdoor trees and plants inside.

Isabelle's weekend visit was Zach's last attempt to circumvent additional expenditures without handling the matter directly. He was counting on her and planned to be in close communication over the next few days. Zach and Amone were more than happy to assist Isabelle with her increasingly willful daughter in exchange for Isabelle handling the difficult conversations with Harriet.

Isabelle had not yet made her way out of the greater Portland area when Zach phoned. When she saw his name come across her dash via the Bluetooth signal she answered. "How's Winnie?"

"Fine. We got delayed by a dog that had been hit by a car," Zach said.

"Oh, that's terrible."

"It's why there are leash laws, Izz," Zach retorted.

"I know but it's still sad," Isabelle said.

"So about Harriet," Zach started. "I need for you to find out if she's signed any agreements to start work on this atrium. Can you believe that? A freaking atrium? I don't even have an atrium and my house is worth two million dollars," Zach said, exasperated.

"You know how she loves her plants. They remind her of mom, Zach. I think this whole thing has been her way to reconnect with her sister in some way. Can we really fault her for that?"

"Lord, Izz. Let's get her a nice photo album or something. I'm all about making her comfortable and happy as she gets older but she's spent over two hundred thousand dollars on that property in the last three years. At some point we have to draw the line. Now I'm counting on you, this weekend, to help her see a better way," Zach said emphatically.

"And how exactly do you expect me to do that?"

"Whatever you women say to each other to produce all those good feelings and help each other make sense of everything," Zach said.

"You are so freaking condescending and offensive sometimes. Spit it out. What are you implying," Isabelle said.

"We've been over this. Like a hundred times. You're going to say, 'Aunt Harriet, the property is not worth the money you're sinking into it. It's not a good investment. I care about you too much to let you keep doing this.' That's what you say, Izz."

"What if she says she doesn't care? What if she says it's her money and she'll spend it how she damn well pleases?"

"You need to make her care," Zach instructed.

"What if she says she's going to die and she can't take the money with her?"

"You explain, gently, in a womanly way that what she's doing is irresponsible."

"In a what? What the heck does that mean, a womanly way?" Isabelle snapped.

"You assured me you could handle this and now I don't know. I need to be able to trust you to help her understand that we want what's best for her. Can you manage this?" Zach asked.

Isabelle was becoming increasingly frustrated with her brother. *I don't need your psycho-babble crap. Why do I have to be the one who handles all his dirty work?* "Zach, I'm in traffic. I need to call you back." Without waiting for his response, Isabelle touched the button to disconnect.

No sooner had the phone disconnected than the phone was ringing again. It was Zach. "I told you I'm in traffic," Isabelle reiterated in lieu of her usual greeting.

"Let's talk this out so you feel comfortable with the message," Zach said.

"I've got it. Bye," Isabelle said. She disconnected again. Isabelle laughed as she hung up, relishing the moment of getting under her brother's skin.

The alert went off on her phone that she received a Facebook instant message. *Oh my gosh, you are so relentless, Zach. Leave me alone.* Isabelle picked up her phone to confirm that her brother was badgering her, only to see it wasn't him. There was a patrol car beside her and the officer looked over just as she switched off her phone. *No, no, no. Not a ticket now.* The officer turned on his lights. *I have the worst luck.*

Isabelle was relieved to see he was in pursuit of another car, but it was a reminder to her to leave her phone alone in traffic. *Okay, maybe I don't have the worst luck.* She smiled. Isabelle turned on her XM satellite to Doctor Radio for health and medical information. It was her favorite talk format since neither sports nor politics appealed much to her.

A few miles outside of Ellensburg, the signal came on her dash of a tire pressure issue. It was the rear passenger side wheel. *Seriously.* She pulled over to the side of Interstate-90, and got out to take a look. Sure enough the tire was half flat. *This had to happen on an interstate with my girl in the car.*

Isabelle got back into the driver's seat and called roadside assistance. The towing company informed her she was second on their call list and they would be there within thirty minutes. *I guess that's not bad. It would be two hours outside of Portland.*

While she waited for the response team, Isabelle checked her phone. She didn't have anything else to do. The Facebook message that came in took her breath away. She just stared at the name. She had looked him up but never friended him. And she knew Facebook wasn't like LinkedIn in that people could see who had been scoping their profile. *Have we been thinking of each other at the same time?*

She opened the app. She tried to view the profile without accepting the friend request but he had it locked down. Hope was asleep in the backseat. She slept through everything. If she had been Grace, she would have been awake the entire trip, asking questions Isabelle couldn't answer.

Isabelle looked again at the name: Masingho Lobato. It was her first great love in college and right after. This was the man she first thought she would marry, if only he hadn't returned to Portugal and misplaced his passport. *I should have returned to Portugal with him.* During some of the rockier times in her marriage to Arnie, Isabelle had been tempted to reconnect with her one-time love. But she always resisted. She honored her commitment to her marriage, and to her, that meant never even reaching out to greet temptation innocently. And here he was, reaching out to her, requesting to friend her. *What does he want? Why connect with me now?* Isabelle's mind was flooded with questions. *Does he know I'm single? Did he hear about Arnie's death?*

Isabelle didn't know if she wanted to reconnect with Masingho. So long as he was just a memory, she could remember him the way she chose. The beliefs she held about him and their relationship were exclusively what she wanted them to be and not necessarily an authentic representation of who he actually became over the years. And yet, a part of her – a significant part of her – did want to accept his friend request. She had been lonely since Arnie died. Her focus had been on her family – the girls, Harriet, Zach and Amone. There hadn't been anyone to sweep her off her feet, and she missed that. *Is it possible Masingho would do that again? Is it possible to still have the life we once talked about together?*

She inhaled deeply, as if she were getting ready to jump out of a plane on a skydiving exhibition. *There's no going back if I do this.* And then with her right index finger, she touched the confirm button. The gap of half a lifetime closed with one simple move. Just like that, the man she wondered about for so long was suddenly back in her life. It was an enormous move for her to wrap her head around.

For a few moments, Isabelle found herself unreservedly immersed in Masingho's profile, to the point that nothing else in her world existed. *He's real. He's not in my imagination anymore.* Many of the answers to questions she had wondered about for years were suddenly spread before her, like a confusing array of salads and casseroles at a family potluck on the Fourth of July. No drum roll. No fan fair. No build up or anticipation. If anything, she felt like a girl who had wanted something for so long, and then one day, out of nowhere, long past the moment she relinquished the expectation of ever achieving it, a stranger handed her a key that unlocked a magic wardrobe.

Isabelle truly had no idea what to expect. But she knew she couldn't wait to explore the profile of this man who no doubt would have seemed ordinary and borderline dull to nearly any other stranger on the planet. To be fair, Masingho was not a gorgeous man. He had a large, wide nose, curly brown hair with gray swirled throughout, and glasses that did not especially complement the shape of his face. But none of that mattered to Isabelle.

A smile crawled across her face as she scrolled through the most important things first. *He's single. He's a dad. His daughter looks sweet. She loves him. She has his eyes. He's goofy and has fun with her. He still lives in Portugal. He works in software. Financial software. He always did love the stock market.* She scrolled through nearly a hundred photos, pinching her fingers apart to look more closely at some. This viewing exercise left her wanting more. *He must be divorced. There are no pictures of his wife. Or ex-wife. Maybe he's a widower. Oh Masingho. What does it mean that you reached out now?*

Isabelle looked up from her phone and stared forward through the windshield. Time was non-existent, it seemed to her, at this moment. She inhaled long, slow, deep breaths, feeling her chest expand and her diaphragm rise. And then she exhaled, just as slowly and every bit as completely. She stared ahead at the trees and the road, the clouds and the sky, but she didn't see any of them. It was in this moment that Isabelle experienced another first. *So this is what it feels like to just be.* Oddly enough, seeing him again brought her a sense of calm, but not a sense of purpose. She felt strangely detached from the outcome. No plan. No anticipation. No worries. No regrets. Isabelle sat peacefully on the side of the highway, as calm as if she were utterly alone in a small boat on calm waters with no other living soul around for miles. Just a girl and her phone in a car with a flat tire.

But she wasn't alone. She had her daughter in the car sleeping, and it was getting dark. Her gas tank indicator was sitting on a quarter full and roadside assistance was later than they promised. *Where is that stupid tow truck?* Hope started to fuss. She had been sleeping and was just waking up. "We'll be to Yia Yia's house soon, honey," she said, hoping to reassure the child.

When she looked in her rearview mirror, she saw that a

pick-up had pulled behind her and a man was getting out of his car and walking toward her driver's side door. This wasn't a police officer and he didn't show up with a tow truck. She stayed calm but wished he'd go away. Help was already on the way. The figure walking toward her was a tall man wearing jeans and boots. He looked strong – stronger than her. *I'm sure this is just someone who wants to help.* Isabelle looked back at Hope in the backseat. "I'm hungry," the little girl announced. Without missing a beat, Isabelle opened a small bag of crackers and handed them to the child.

Why is the tow truck taking so long? Should I call Zach? Yes, I will call Zach.

She called her brother and the call went straight to voicemail just as the stranger arrived at her window. She didn't want to look at him. She put her window down about an inch, and without looking the man in the face she informed him, "I've already called for help. Roadside assistance will be here any minute. Thank you for stopping but you can go."

"It's getting dark. Do you have flares or anything?" the man asked.

Like I drive around with flares in my car? "No, but I've called for help. They'll be here any minute," she said, trying to balance being polite with also being safe.

"I've got water in my truck. Do you need some water?" he asked. Now Isabelle was getting annoyed. She knew that being an exit away from a small town probably lent itself to a modicum of safety not assured in a city but she still felt vulnerable, less for herself than for her daughter in the car. She looked back at Hope. Her eyes were open wide and she didn't take them off the stranger. If Isabelle could have driven away, she would have. Everything inside of her wanted to. But then she wouldn't have been waiting for help. "Do you want me to give you a ride into town? It's okay. Come with me. I'll take you to the Shell station," he volunteered.

Isabelle was increasingly terrified. She wasn't going to let him know this though. *I'm not accepting a ride from a stranger.* She faced him squarely to show him she wasn't afraid, and to let him also know that he was dangerously close to crossing painfully into her comfort zone. She raised her right hand and pointed to him when she spoke, like a teacher pointing out a lesson in a classroom. *Back off buddy.* "Look, I know you mean well, but I'm a single woman with a baby and I've told you I called roadside assistance. If you want, you can call the police and report a car on the side of the road but I'm not letting you in or going anywhere with you. Do I make myself clear?" She scowled her face forcing her eyebrows together, hoping this would send a distinct message: *if he had improper intentions he was messing with the wrong gal.*

The man was completely taken back. He looked at her like a small town farmer who had just been accused of stealing his neighbor's pig. He had a confused look on his face, which won him no sympathy from Isabelle. When he first opened his mouth, nothing came out. Finally he spoke. Just one word. "Isabelle?"

CHAPTER 3

“**I** know you,” Isabelle said. She couldn't believe her eyes. *What?* “You're that guy from the beach. You bought me a cup of coffee. OMG.” What an unexpected coincidence this was for both of them, despite the fact that Owen had been hoping for months to run into the feisty red-head again.

“You dyed your hair. Red,” he said.

“I was ready for something different and it seemed like a safe adventure.”

“It's nice,” he said as he titled his head and winked awkwardly. Isabelle didn't really know how to respond to his mildly self-conscious mannerisms, so she pinched her leg with a hand hidden from his view, and smiled. *That guy.*

She wasn't sure if she liked his awkwardness or not, but she wanted to get Hope and herself off the freeway. “I've called roadside assistance, but, uh, it's taking longer.” Isabelle said. “I have my daughter in the backseat.” Owen looked back at Hope, who was fully awake.

“Hope, this is a friend of mommy's.” *He's not really a friend. Why would I call him a friend? I met him once. He could be a serial killer for all I know.* She looked at him again, more skeptically. *No, he's fine.*

“Let's get you two settled into my truck and call the towing company to see how far out they are. Sound good?" Owen asked.

"Sounds good. Thanks," Isabelle said. Owen made sure there was no traffic coming before opening the car door to let Isabelle out. Isabelle also checked. She trusted him but not enough to potentially hop out into traffic without a second glance.

Isabelle walked around to the passenger side and unbuckled Hope from her car seat. "Hey baby girl. We're going to wait in Owen's car for the tow truck to come," Isabelle told Hope. Hope started to cry and fuss. This was unusual, but it was late and the wind blew Hope's hair in her face. Isabelle grabbed her blanket and her stuffed elephant, Rory.

A gentleman, Owen opened the passenger door on his truck and offered to hold Hope while Isabelle climbed up into the cab. For a snap-second Isabelle wasn't comfortable handing over her daughter, but she didn't know if this was intuition or just a normal motherly response. When she got in, she immediately reached for Hope and Owen lifted her up. "Thank you," Isabelle said. *I should have left her with Zach and Amone.* Isabelle couldn't have known she would have a flat tire, but she often went over alternate scenarios in her mind.

Isabelle wrapped Hope in the blanket and the toddler nestled into Isabelle's chest, Rory by her side, and self-soothed by sucking her thumb. It was a habit Isabelle was trying to break, but she wasn't going to address it this moment. She knew Hope was already uncomfortable enough. Just as she got settled the tow truck showed up. As Isabelle started to move to get down, Owen stopped her. "Hey, I'll take care of this. No worries," he said. She thought about offering him her insurance information, but he said he'd take care of it and she let him. It felt nice to be cared for, even if it was by a stranger who was just responding to a random woman in need of car help.

After about ten minutes, Isabelle watched the tow truck

driver load her car – and everything in it – onto his flatbed truck. *Uh, this is not okay. I need my stuff. I need Hope's stuff. How are we going to get to Harriet's?* No sooner had a ton of questions started rapidly flowing through her mind than Owen opened the driver's side door and climbed up into the driver's seat next to her with answers.

"So we're going to meet him over at the Ellensburg Tire Center," Owen stated unequivocally. "He has some paperwork for you to sign and you can get your stuff out of the car. I'll call them in the morning and let you know when it's ready to pick up," he said. *Wow! Just like that it's handled.* Isabelle liked this quite a lot. She was used to being the person who had to handle everything for everyone else and it was so nice to have someone handle something for her. Suddenly, Owen seemed a lot less awkward and a lot more interesting.

"Thank you," she enthusiastically grinned in appreciation. She played with her hair, twirling the ends between her middle and forefingers, the way she often did when she wanted a man to remember her.

After Isabelle signed the paperwork and pointed to the bags she wanted, Owen put them in his truck and asked her where she was planning to spend the night. *Oh dear, I hope I didn't give him the wrong impression.* "We're staying with my aunt," Isabelle blurted out, with a noticeable nod, and a more pronounced tone than she intended. She didn't want him getting any crazy ideas.

Owen looked at her without saying a word.

"I may have met you in Hawaii but I'm not that kind of girl," she laid out her boundaries.

"The kind of girl who would give me the address for where you would like to be dropped off?" Owen asked. He acted like he was confused but he was inwardly pleased that he rattled her.

"Wow. I'm sorry," she said. They both laughed. "Harriet's address. Of course." She closed her eyes and dropped her head. "I am sorry. And embarrassed. But mostly sorry." They both continued laughing.

"It's totally cool. But I'm glad we got that established."

"Yes," Isabelle said, still embarrassed.

"I mean, that I clearly don't read minds." Owen laughed.

"Yes, that too," Isabelle blinked her eyes really tight and sighed. "I'm really sorry. You've been nothing but a gentleman." She gave him the address and he plugged it into his phone GPS.

"Normally, I could give you directions. I'm here often. Too often," she said.

"It's okay. Siri's got this one," he said, just as his phone told him to take a left in a quarter of a mile.

Harriet's house was close to town so the drive from the tire shop only took a few minutes. "Wow," he said when they pulled up.

"Yes, it's a little unexpected," Isabelle said. "She definitely wins the prize for the most money sunk into a little house, perhaps in the entire Northwest." Isabelle laughed. "She's got plans for an atrium out the back, unless I'm able to change her mind this weekend."

"That's a mighty fine fence," Owen said.

"It's like a wall," Isabelle said.

"Like a fortress," Owen added. They both laughed. Isabelle was truly enjoying herself in a way she hadn't for a very long time – at least since Arnie's death but possibly for some time before.

"So you're kinda an unlikely superhero," Isabelle teased. "Rushing in. Saving the…"

"Damsel in distress," Owen finished her sentence.

"I was going to say, 'Saving the day,' but I suppose being stranded at dusk on the freeway possibly qualifies me as a modern day damsel in distress," Isabelle said, with a smile.

"Uh yeah," he said, blushing. This caught Isabelle off guard. While technically her flirting was intentional, she didn't intend for him to take her seriously, which it appeared he had.

I need to lighten this up a bit.

"Well, at least you're not passing yourself off as a Duck tonight," she said with a smile, raising her eyebrows and biting her lower lip as she tilted her head to the right.

"You're a bit of a mystery, Isabelle," he paused waiting for her to finish his sentence with her last name. She didn't finish his sentence. She knew that's what he wanted so she intentionally didn't fill in the blanks for him.

"You're not the first man to accuse me of that," she playfully returned the ball. She had taken him so off-guard that he had to be extra vigilant not to let on that he knew any more about her than she shared. The wheels inside his mind were turning and for a moment he had a strange look on his face, which did not go unnoticed by her.

"What's going on in there?" she asked.

"Where?" Owen asked.

"That fun little head of yours. It's like you want to say something but the cat's got your tongue."

Owen debated telling her about the ring, Arnie's ring, but he didn't know how to blurt it out without sounding like a weird stalker. *Hey, so crazy thing. I have your ring. Or maybe, I think you're really pretty. Do you want your dead husband's ring back?* As Owen quickly played through so many possible conversations in his mind, none of the options sounded like they might actually endear her to him. The last thing he wanted was to freak her out. And if he didn't tell her, how and when would he? He held onto the information for the time being. He was sure the right words would come at the right time.

"Owen?" Isabelle rested her left hand on his arm and shook him just a bit. *Wow! Nice arms.* She was impressed that a man in his forties had biceps like that. But she too decided to keep that to herself for the time being.

"Sorry. I was thinking about something," he said.

"Apparently something confusing?" she asked.

"Uhm, yes, my schedule for tomorrow."

"Excuse me?" Isabelle wasn't sure what he was talking about. *His schedule? His Saturday schedule?*

"I was going to offer to give you a ride to the tire shop tomorrow, to get your tire fixed, but I don't remember my schedule, exactly." He covered.

"Oh, don't worry about it. My aunt can take me. It's no big deal. You saved me from a potentially reckless driver on the freeway so one rescue is good," she said.

"Well, it was my pleasure," he said.

"At least let me buy you a cup of coffee, tomorrow, or when you know your schedule. I'm here all weekend," she said. "Do you lecture on Saturdays?"

"Uh no," he said, without immediate clarification.

"Okay then, well, perhaps I'll run into you, again," she said.

"Well I know where you live. Should I just drive by or do you have a phone number? That might be easier." Owen tried to lighten things back up with a laugh.

"Yes, let me give you that number. Here, I can type my information into your phone contacts if you want," she offered.

"Sure," he said, handing her his iPhone.

When she finished inputting her contact info, she handed his phone back, making sure to touch hands. She immediately looked away. She could see Harriet in the window watching them. "There's Harriet," she said, waving. Harriet waved back. *Oh there will be questions about this.* "I grew up in this house," Isabelle said.

"I remember," Owen replied.

"You remember? What do you mean?" she asked, skeptically. Owen seemed familiar from the moment they first met, but she could never place him.

"You mentioned it over coffee in Maui," Owen covered.

"Oh," Isabelle said, again caught off guard. "I didn't remember telling you that."

"You said you grew up here when you were a kid, and then your family moved, I think to Oregon." Owen said. Isabelle was sure she had not told him that. She wouldn't have said that her family moved. She wouldn't have talked about this with a stranger. Her neck started to feel warm. *Who is this man? Does he know me? Did he set out to meet me?* Isabelle had a lot of questions, but with Harriet opening the front door and starting down the sidewalk toward the truck, Isabelle would not get the answers she needed that night.

Seeing this, he hopped out of his side of the truck and immediately went around to open Isabelle's door. By this time, Harriet was at the truck and Isabelle needed to explain. As Isabelle began to explain their relationship to Harriet, in the most simple and generic way, Owen carried their belongings to the front porch.

"We got a flat tire. My friend Owen came along while we were waiting for roadside assistance. Owen, this is Harriet. Harriet, Owen. Owen took Hope and me over to the tire shop to get our stuff and brought us here," Isabelle tried to act like none of this was a big deal. In reality, everything about it was a big deal now. She wished Harriet hadn't just walked outside and interrupted their conversation. Isabelle had given Owen all of her information but she didn't even know his last name. *Professor who? Darn it, Harriet. Why didn't you just wait for me inside?*

Isabelle was glad she had given Owen her Hushed account phone number. At least when she was finished with business in Ellensburg she could disable it and be done with everyone here, including this fake-Duck, non-surfer, whoever he was. She wanted to ask him his last name, but she had already told Harriet they were friends and she didn't want to throw out any red flags that might spark an in-depth conversation with questions from Harriet she didn't have answers for. She just had to go with it at this point.

"Thank you again, for everything Owen," Isabelle said. She wasn't sure if she should hug him goodbye. She was torn between not wanting to touch him and very much wanting to feel his strong, tight, muscular arms once more. He reached out to hug her and without resisting she felt herself drawing into him. "Call me tomorrow. I want to make good on that cup of coffee I owe you," Isabelle said. She couldn't care less about a cup of coffee. But she was determined to figure out his story and from where she really knew him.

Meanwhile, Harriet was about to launch a thousand questions her direction, and she needed time to formulate enough of a story with enough answers to throw Harriet off the trail of truth.

Although Harriet was critical of Isabelle growing up, in her role as a surrogate mother, even Isabelle had to admit she was an absolute dream of a doting grandparent to Hope and Grace. Isabelle was tired and her mind was running wild in too many directions to fully consider. She sat down on the sofa and forgot to take off Hope's jacket.

Harriet stepped in effortlessly without being asked. She unzipped the jacket and checked if she was hungry. When she nodded she was, Harriet took Hope into the kitchen, thirty feet away and lifted her up onto the high leather stool with substantial arms at the kitchen bar. "I thought you might be, sweetheart. I have goldfish crackers right here just for you," Harriet said. "Do you want some juice or some milk?" Listening to Harriet lovingly care for Hope delighted Isabelle to her core.

"Juice," Hope said.

"Did you say please?" Isabelle called out from the other room.

"Juice please," Hope corrected.

"So who is this Owen again?" Harriet asked. *Oh dear God, not already.*

"Just an acquaintance. He stopped to help and I recognized him. Otherwise I wouldn't have accepted a ride, clearly," Isabelle said.

"Why didn't you call me?" Harriet asked.

"Well, I called roadside assistance. I didn't think to call anyone else, really. He just showed up."

"And how do you know him?" Harriet questioned.

"Gosh, how do I know him?" Isabelle was stalling.

"You don't even live here. Have you made friends on the few visits you've made to see me?"

"Well, I've been up a lot more than a few times. What are you saying? Do you feel like I don't visit enough? Would you like for me to visit more?" Isabelle was trying to change the subject.

"Honey, I love having you visit. Remind me tomorrow to show you my new herb garden I'm getting started outside to bring in this winter." *Oh good it worked. Did it work? Think positive, Isabelle.*

"I've never really had any luck growing basil inside for long so we'll see if it's different this year," Harriet continued.

"So which herbs did you add to the garden and are you sure they will all live?" Isabelle needed to solidly secure a new conversation subject and what better than to fall back on Harriet's love of plants and all green living things?

"I always seem to do well with parsley, if I use enough of it to keep it regenerating, and the rosemary does well, which is great at Thanksgiving. My cilantro usually dies. The sage does okay – not great but okay. The oregano does okay but the thyme not so much. Do you want me to start a garden for you?" Harriet asked.

What on earth would I do with that?

"I'd love that," Isabelle said. *Yes, this is what we need. A project to do together that doesn't involve my personal life.* Isabelle felt modestly hopeful.

"I can't wait for you to see my plans for the atrium," Harriet shared excitedly. *Oh that's right. The atrium.* Isabelle almost forgot about the atrium and her weekend assignment from Zach. Isabelle wasn't entirely sure how to dissuade Harriet from building the atrium. But she knew Zach was counting on her to help Aunt Harriet understand that she was investing *a king's ransom into a beggar's purse*, in his words.

When Isabelle looked up, Hope was asleep, mouth open, drooling, her little face on the counter, pressed into her yellow crackers. *My precious baby girl.* Isabelle tipped her head to the side and smiled at her daughter. "She sleeps a lot for a child," Isabelle said to Harriet, hoping to elicit a concerned response.

"It's ten o'clock at night. Of course she's tired," Harriet observed. "Plus, she's still teething and looks to me like she's going through a growth spurt. I bet she's at least an inch taller than she was in Maui. Kids grow when they sleep."

"I suppose," Isabelle said. Isabelle had never heard that before. "I'm going to go put her down for the night. Should we measure her and see if she's taller in the morning?" Isabelle said, joking. Harriet was always so literal that of course she responded as if Isabelle had asked a serious question. "Harriet, I'm kidding." She sighed when she had to explain herself.

"You can be lucky you aren't having to rock and cajole her to sleep only to have her spring back into action a few hours later. If Arnie were here he could probably tell you more about how Grace was at this age." *Arnie? Are you out of your mind?* It was all Isabelle could do to bite her lip and not respond. She had been the primary caregiver to Grace; Arnie, God rest his soul, was too involved in fantasy football and other random hobbies that didn't support the family to even know what Grace was doing. Isabelle counted to ten in her head.

In trying to be helpful, Harriet sometimes made Isabelle feel like climbing the walls. *Isabelle, do you want to get into an argument tonight? Do you want to go there? No. No you don't. So zip it – and let it go.* Isabelle frequently got through life by engaging these self-talk vignettes in her own head.

Isabelle walked over to her little girl and picked her up gently, rocked her at first and then walked out of the room with the child in her arms. *If I go to bed now, I won't have to explain any more about Owen until the morning. Dang, I don't even know his last name.* She didn't want to tell Harriet about meeting him in Maui, because her luck, Harriet would remember the one day Isabelle went surfing and came home late. Isabelle could already anticipate Harriet questioning this. Isabelle often felt like she had so much explaining to do around Harriet. She knew it was because Harriet cared – and was nosey – perhaps equally caring and nosey.

Isabelle considered herself to be a private person and nearly any amount of meddlesome questions pushed Isabelle out of her comfort zone quickly. Fortunately for Isabelle, back in Portland, Zach never seemed interesting in anything outside of his own world. Almost Zach's polar opposite in this way, Amone had such an acute level of emotional intelligence that she could read Isabelle's earliest signals of discomfort regarding most topics and quickly change the subject.

Isabelle decided she would try to find Owen's last name before morning, and come up with some plausible explanation for how she knew him – plausible-sounding anyway, as she obviously couldn't tell Harriet the truth. She debated even returning to say goodnight to Harriet – a known night owl – after tucking Hope into bed, to avoid getting prematurely baited into a conversation about Owen. Isabelle wasn't a good liar with preparation, and she was positively terrible without.

Just as she was deciding what to do, her phone buzzed. It was a text from Zach. *How did dinner go with Harriet?*

Funny you should ask, she typed back.

Were you able to sway her?

I just got here. I had a flat tire.

Glad you're okay. I'll check in with you tomorrow.

"Seriously?" Isabelle found herself saying aloud, which of course Harriet overheard and responded by coming into the guest room to check on her.

"Is everything okay?" Harriet asked.

"Oh, yes. I just got a text from Zach."

"Is he okay?"

He's fine. He's just Zach being Zach."

"What does that mean?" Harriet asked. It wasn't like Isabelle could really tell her what he said or about their plan to sway her to more conservative spending choices.

"You know how men are. It's nothing," Isabelle reassured

their aunt. *Why do I have to fix all the world's problems?*

"I made some tea for you. Do you want to come out to the living room or shall I bring it in here?" Harriet asked.

It was just like Harriet to do something thoughtful when Isabelle had other plans – plans to get online and then go to bed. But it wasn't like she could say no. Her only choice was to join her aunt in the small parlor or have her aunt join her in the bedroom – and either way, hope the conversation didn't lead back to the professor tonight. She had to think on her feet.

"I'm going to wash my face and I'll be out in two minutes," Isabelle promised.

"Great," Harriet said, turning to walk away. *One cup of tea.* Then, suddenly, Isabelle remembered something she had been meaning to talk to Harriet about for some time. *This might be the perfect opportunity to get some answers. I'm going to get to the bottom of this one way or another.*

Ever since they returned from Maui, Grace had been having a recurring nightmare. Each time, slightly different details came out but there were two key elements that were always the same, and Isabelle saw something on Harriet's face that made her feel certain that Harriet knew more than she was sharing. Harriet guarded her own secrets even more closely than Isabelle guarded hers, which meant Isabelle needed to get as much information out of Harriet without giving up a bargaining chip in the process. It was likely Harriet had her own investigation going on simultaneous to the puzzle Isabelle was piecing together on her end.

Isabelle slipped on a gray, long-sleeve pullover and yoga pants and stepped out to the small kitchen where Harriet had hot chamomile tea ready. "How have you been?" Isabelle asked as she entered the room.

"Great. I feel alive here," Harriet said.

"You like Ellensburg that much?" Isabelle questioned.

"I grew up here. Even though I've spent most of my life in Portland, this is where my memories and dreams originated. As I get older, I think about mom and dad, Joy and," Harriet stopped. She started to get emotional and quickly suppressed it.

"You can tell me," Isabelle said.

"There are some things a woman doesn't even admit to herself, let alone share."

"That's ridiculous," Isabelle admonished.

"What good does it do to focus on sad or negative things. It's not like talking about them will change things," Harriet said.

"Look Harriet, I love you and I fought for you to live. I sat by your bed and cheered you. I worked with Carrie and the other doctors to help get you the care you needed. I even prayed for you. I hadn't prayed in years, until the morning I mysteriously found myself in a hospital chapel, lighting a candle and begging God to let you live," Isabelle opened up. "You drive me bat- shit crazy. You never respect my personal space. You ask me a thousand questions I don't have the answers for. You're not al- ways that nice – and then out of the blue, you're unexpectedly thoughtful, and I don't always know what to say to communi- cate with you."

"What do you mean I'm not thoughtful? I'm always thoughtful," Harriet corrected.

"But despite your flaws, I love you madly."

"Despite my flaws? I don't have any real flaws. I've never been arrested. I don't abuse alcohol. I have a glass of wine here and there, but I've never smoked pot, even though it's legal in Washington now." Harriet started her rebuttal, and she was just getting started. Isabelle tried not to smile when she imagined that a little marijuana might not be so bad for Harriet. *Perhaps pot would calm her some. Maybe prevent these conversations in the future.* Isabelle worked hard to not smile at what would have been a highly inopportune time.

"You're right. It is legal." Isabelle made a joke, which of course fell flat to Harriet.

"I help those less fortunate. I volunteer at KVH. I really try to bring a smile to others, to leave my small corner of the world better than it was." Harriet assured her niece. Harriet was appalled to learn that Isabelle saw her as less than perfect. Isabelle's eyes began to gloss over. This was exactly what Isabelle wanted to avoid. Well, this and having her bring up the professor again. Isabelle scratched her head. *Oh dear God, this was going to be one quick cup of tea.* Harriet continued to talk. She had a gift for cycling through a dozen topics without even pausing to take a breath. "It has been my absolute pleasure in life to sacrifice in every way I could, to give you and Zach the very best opportunities in life." Harriet finally stopped.

"I know. Thank you," Isabelle jumped in. She wanted to run away from this conversation. Not walk, but run. *At least she hasn't brought up Owen. Yet.*

"Did I fail you? Was I not there for you in elementary school and junior high when your had band practice at six-thirty in the morning because the buses didn't run that early?"

"Harriet, stop. For a moment."

This fell on deaf ears. Harriet kept talking while Isabelle zoned out. In her own thought bubble, Isabelle imagined banging her head up and down on the table over and over. When she tuned back in, Harriet was still explaining herself.

"Did I not convince Frank that you should have a dog, two cats and a lizard?" *Actually, the lizard belonged to Zach.* Isabelle wanted to interrupt her aunt to correct her about the lizard but she knew that would be a really bad idea at this point. "And you reward me by telling me I'm mean? How could you ever say that to me?" Harriet was completely appalled.

I'm probably not getting any real answers tonight.

"Okay, reset," Isabelle said, crossing her hands together to form a time-out-T. "I'm sorry I said you weren't thoughtful. What I intended to say was that despite our differences, you are one of the five most important people in the world to me and when you are gone, I'm the only person who will in essence be able to carry on your legacy. So I need for you to trust me enough to help me figure out some really important things while you're still here and while you still can. Will you do that for me?" Isabelle asked.

"Well, I don't know why you would want my help if the legacy you think I'm leaving behind is being mean." Harriet was not in a position to listen to Isabelle. Harriet was rarely in a position to listen to anyone, but even less, in this moment, to listen to Isabelle right now. Isabelle's tea was gone and she wasn't sure she had the endurance to go another round tonight. It was exhausting picking every single word perfectly so as not to ruffle Harriet's feathers.

She needed Harriet's help in getting to the bottom of what was going on with Grace. She knew the nightmares were significant and she knew that despite what Harriet was saying, Harriet knew more than she was letting on. If only Isabelle could ask Harriet these things in a straight-forward text, like Zach did with her.

Isabelle rinsed out her cup and set it in the dishwasher. She turned to walk away and then stopped suddenly after taking three steps. "Grace is having nightmares about you being in a fire and searching for a book," Isabelle said, as she spun around to see the look on Harriet's face. "What do you think this means?" Isabelle asked.

"How would I know? I don't analyze dreams. I'm not a

psychologist. I can't possibly know what it means," Harriet said.

"The look on your face when she had this dream in Maui said otherwise." It may have been confrontational but Isabelle had no choice but to go there. It was almost eleven o'clock and Isabelle was prepared to stay up all night to get her questions about Grace answered. While she may not have been the most in-tune and responsive parent the last three years, Isabelle knew these dreams were significant and she needed to figure this out for her daughter. For all the things Isabelle hadn't been able to give Grace, this was one things she was determined to see through.

"I've never been in a fire. I don't know what the dreams are about," Harriet said. She shifted her weight from one foot to the other, almost nervously.

"Great. I hope you're never in a fire. That would be frightening and potentially devastating. What do you know about a book? Why are you looking for this book? I need to understand what this is about." Isabelle didn't mince words.

Harriet inhaled a deep breath of air, reacting to it almost like a gulp of ice water when it was too hot outside to adjust to a temperature change. She couldn't help but express a natural and spontaneous physical reaction. She had to come clean. "I don't know, exactly," Harriet said. "I'm not sure the book I'm looking for even exists, or even if it's a book at all. I just know I'm looking for something and I'll know it when I find it."

"What does your gut tell you?"

"What I'm looking for will answer the questions I've had for many years. I suspect it's a book, but whatever it is, it is special. And finding it is important to me," Harriet said quietly, after she softened her tone a bit.

CHAPTER 4

"**W**hat's the name of the book you're looking for and why is it so important?" Isabelle asked. She reached for her iPhone and pulled up her Amazon app before Harriet could even respond. Isabelle was poised to type the name into the search feature.

"It's not a book you're going to find on Amazon, or at any other retailer," Harriet said. "I'm the last living person who ever knew it existed."

"I don't understand." There was no sleeping now. Harriet had Isabelle's full attention.

"This is going to require a longer conversation than I have energy for tonight," Harriet said. "I will tell you what I know but because you're going to have questions, I need to feel physically strong enough to have this discussion. I don't feel up to it tonight. We need to continue this conversation later," Harriet said.

"No. No. No. We're not going to continue this conversation later. Look, either this is important enough that it will keep me from sleeping, or this is another one of your teasers where you make me believe there's a landmine five feet away and it turns out to be a lost button on the floor. This book is giving my twelve-year-old daughter recurring nightmares. You're going to tell me tonight what it is."

"I'm just sure my sister's diary is in this house." Immediately Harriet started to silently sob uncontrollably, to the point she couldn't speak for several minutes. She bowed her head and the crown of her scalp bobbed with each inhaled breath. Isabelle had never seen Harriet so emotional. "I've looked everywhere for it. I don't know that it's here anymore. I don't know if a renter threw it out over the years. I honestly don't know where it is but Grace is right that I have been searching for it. I just can't bring myself to let it go," Harriet said.

"Well, I guess that makes sense on some level." Isabelle was disappointed by the news. She would have loved to get her hands on her mother's diary, but it didn't make sense why Grace was dreaming about Harriet trying to find it. "Let's take a step back. What could she have written that would have been so important forty years ago? I mean, Harriet, I've never seen you like this. There is either something consequential in that diary, or at the very least, you have a reason to believe there could be." Isabelle stared at Harriet, leaning into the counter, arms crossed in front of her chest.

"I never read the diary. I respected her privacy. I looked for it after the car accident. Do you remember seeing it as a child?" Harriet asked.

Isabelle paused to think back. "I don't." Isabelle didn't know what to make of this. Of course she would have loved to hold something so dear to her mom – to read her mom's thoughts and see her handwriting. As much as Isabelle truly had come to love Harriet as a mom, a part of her still longed to know her biological mother, Joy. Isabelle felt torn and perplexed. It wasn't like Harriet to lie. Evade the truth – now Harriet was a master at that. There was so much Isabelle knew Harriet had never shared with her. But Isabelle believed Harriet when she said that she had never read this diary. Still, by normal measures, Harriet's reaction tonight was utterly incomprehensible. *Unless Harriet knows something more.*

Isabelle believed that Harriet had to suspect there was something in the diary that, by Harriet's reaction, had to be some sort of a game-changer that could potentially upend all their lives. Isabelle didn't have any answers and didn't even know what questions to ask. So she tried to figure out a logical and reasonable response. *I don't think we're going to figure this out tonight.* Her response for the time being was to let it go and try to get some sleep. They had a busy weekend ahead and this would need to take its place with the other pressing matters on Isabelle's mind and to-do list.

She quickly scanned her phone to see she had twenty-nine unread emails, two missed calls, one private message via Facebook and of course she still needed to learn more about the professor who also seemed to hold his own chest of secrets. Instead of addressing any of them, she powered her phone down and crawled into bed. *I am not going to solve any world problems tonight.*

◆ ◆ ◆

The next morning, Isabelle was awoken by a rooster. He belonged to one of Harriet's neighbors. *Seriously, roosters in the city limits? This would never happen in Portland. What's next?*

Isabelle had never been a morning person, or a terribly tolerant person, although she was actively working on the latter. She really wanted coffee, but thought she better get online and do some snooping around about Owen before she wandered out to the kitchen and Harriet suddenly remembered the man who dropped her off the night before.

She went online to the Central Washington University website and right there under faculty and staff was Dr. Owen Mallinger. Sure enough, he taught Environmental Microbiology 420. Isabelle didn't even know what that meant.

So she did what she always did: she researched it. She researched him and his field of expertise. *The ecology specialization is designed for students interested in basic and applied ecology, including fisheries, wildlife management, forestry, ecological restoration, and conservation biology. Students following this specialization will gain experience in natural history, field research, and experimental design. Potential careers may be found in federal, state, and tribal agencies, or private environmental consulting firms. The ecology faculty strongly suggests that every student augment the single required taxonomy course with an elective second taxonomy course. Students interested in graduate study in ecology should work closely with their advisor to tailor this specialization to their particular field of interest.*

At least she had his full name and could explain what he taught. Next she had to figure out a believable story for how they met. Something simple. Too much detail might look planned. She didn't want to set off any red flags to Harriet. Her goal was to make him a non-issue. At least for now. She liked him more than she wanted to but she wasn't going to let herself fall for him until she figured out on her own if it was safe to do so.

It would have been great if she had even one friend in Ellensburg. She could have said she met him through her friend. That would be simple, and believable. She wouldn't have to know much about him that way. But she didn't have any friends here. She didn't even really have any friends to speak of in Portland. Most of her time was spent with her kids, her brother and Amone, and Carrie. *I have friends. Carrie's a friend. No, she's more of a sister. She has to put up with me for Harriet.* And writing. Now that her first book, her largely surprising breakout novel, had been published and landed on the New York Times best seller list, she had an advance from her publisher on a second, and as such she devoted a great deal of time to writing.

Harriet appeared at Isabelle's door just as Isabelle was

opening Facebook. "I have bacon if you're not on a diet this morning," Harriet said.

Isabelle looked up from her tablet. "I'm always on a diet," she said. She wasn't kidding. "I'd still love a piece of bacon, or two. I need to walk to the tire shop this morning. It's not more than a mile."

"I will take you. Or were you assuming I would stay here and take care of Hope while you ran your errands on your own schedule?" Harriet asked. Comments like this once drove Isabelle crazy because of what they inferred; but over the past several years, since Harriet's stroke and subsequent recovery, Isabelle had learned to receive and respond to them differently.

"That would be great. Thanks, Harriet," Isabelle cheerfully replied. While Isabelle meant this with a pinch of sarcasm, Harriet was oblivious to such nuances. Through the exercise of self-management, over the past year, Isabelle had learned to appreciate Harriet's offers to help without coming unhinged every time Harriet said something in a tone that rubbed her harshly. "I appreciate your help," Isabelle said.

"Any time, dear. I'm here to serve." Harriet replied, before turning around and tootling back to the kitchen. Isabelle watched Harriet walk out of the room.

Isabelle's eyes got big as a wide smile washed across her face. The private message alert she dismissed the night before was from none other than her newest Facebook friend – Masingho Lobato. In the chaos of everything that happened the night before, she actually forgot he unexpectedly reached out to her on social media. *How did I not look at this last night?*

His message was brief. And cryptic. *Hey Isabelle. Long time. Hope you have been well. I'm planning a trip to Seattle for business. Want to meet for dinner? Mas*

Isabelle read and re-read his epigrammatic note. Then she counted the words. Twenty-three. *I have butterflies. How can twenty-three little words do this to me?*

It's been twenty years. What on earth could he possibly want? I wonder if he knows I'm single. She checked how her profile appeared to Masingho as a FB user, and it did indeed list her relationship status as single. *Could he possibly? No. Twenty years later? No. I wonder what he wants.*

She reviewed his profile more carefully than she had in the car waiting for help. Whereas she initially focused on the photos, this time she reviewed the information to form her own picture in her mind. *He lives in Sintra. Where's that?* Isabelle pulled up a map of Portugal and discovered it was west of Lisbon. *I've never even heard of Sintra.* She googled it to see what came up.

Isabelle discovered that Sintra was a popular tourist destination in Portugal. The greeting from the visitors center sounded charming: *We hope that once you arrive in Sintra your time will be taken up exploring the wonderful palaces, castles, monasteries and romantic landscaped gardens, plus the beautiful Estoril coastline nearby.*

Sintra, in Portugal, enjoys a year-round climate that is extremely favourable. Thanks to its position on the western coast of the country, it enjoys fresh breezes that rise off the Atlantic and up into the rolling greenery of the Sintra mountain range. In fact, the weather in Sintra was largely to thank for Portugal's former royal family and many members of the European aristocracy making it their favoured summer retreat – thus building the vast array of magical palaces and castles that line its dramatic hilltops.

"Wow!" she said aloud. *Well if I lived there, I might not want to return to rainy Oregon either. I wonder if he lives in a castle.* Isabelle's mind ran wild imagining the current day life of her former love. *Let's see. It's seven-thirty here so that would make it like three-thirty there. So it's mid-afternoon.* Just then, a green dot popped up by his name indicating he had just logged in and was online with Facebook at the exact same time. She froze and then immediately closed the application. *Maybe he didn't see me. Maybe he didn't know I was online. This is so crazy. I feel like we're twenty-two again and why? This is nuts. But does it mean something?*

Harriet had breakfast ready. Isabelle could smell the delicious whiff of fried bacon permeating throughout the house. It had been so long since Isabelle had smelled, let alone allowed herself to actually enjoy, bacon.

When she stepped outside the bedroom into the parlor, her busy little Hope was physically running circles around the kitchen and small dining room. "She sleeps and then she's a baby kangaroo, hopping about without a moment of still," Isabelle said, about Hope, to Harriet. "Morning sweetheart. Can you come give mama a kiss?" Hope went running to Isabelle. Isabelle had squatted down in an awkward position barely balancing, and Hope nearly knocked her over, smothering her with kisses.

"I'm an airplane," Hope announced to Isabelle.

"Where are you going to fly today, Miss Airplane?" Isabelle asked Hope.

"To the zoo," Hope said.

"What a great idea," Isabelle said. Turning to Harriet, Isabelle asked, "Does Ellensburg have a zoo?"

"Not that I'm aware of," Harriet replied.

"Well, you have roosters," Isabelle said. "Is that even part of the city ordinance?"

"Yes and no. That rooster you referred to is an eight-week-old chick that Madison Winters has in her backyard. She can have up to four chickens, including male chicks until they're four months old. That little thing has been crowing since he was about a week old, if you can believe that," Harriet said.

"I thought they did that to mate or something – like, 'Good morning I'm ready to play.' I don't know," Isabelle said laughing. Play was not the word that first came to mind but she had become solid at self-editing when she was around Harriet.

"Well, Madison has two more months to find her little town crier a new home, and in the spirit of neighborly love I do my level best to just tolerate the little guy for now," Harriet said.

"I would not be tolerating it that long if I lived here, but I won't ruffle any feathers with your neighbors," Isabelle said, hoping Harriet would love the pun. But it flew right over, completely unnoticed. So Isabelle laughed to herself and moved on.

"Madison is a good neighbor and friend, and if the chips were down, I know she'd be there for me. So her rooster wakes me up. My bones ache so much I'd be getting up anyway," Harriet said.

Isabelle marveled at how beautiful Harriet's breakfast table looked. *All this for breakfast? She missed her calling.* It was fit for a diplomat. As elegant as any state dinner. Every plate, glass and utensil in its perfect place. Isabelle felt as if she were dining in an upscale restaurant in Portland or any other exclusive metropolitan club – aside from the dated wall paper and a few too many crystal knick-knacks for her liking. At least it was perfectly ordered, unlike the piles of paper and newspapers that Isabelle found herself cleaning out of her own home periodically.

Harriet served orange juice in half-full, tiny eight ounce old-fashioned glasses that Isabelle thought were probably intended to serve whiskey neat or Bourbon on the rocks with a twist of lemon. It was the sweetest orange juice Isabelle could ever remember drinking. "How much sugar did you add to this?"

"Not a pinch. God made those oranges sweet."

Harriet had a way of making Isabelle laugh with her charming eccentricity.

Ever since the day she encountered the man on the bench, and the night she almost lost Snoopy, Isabelle stopped trying to assume she had all the answers. What a relief it was for her to stop feeling continually offended by Harriet's unorthodox, possibly silly declarations of faith in everyday, ordinary occurrences. *If this is how Harriet sees it, so be it. Who's to say she's wrong?*

Isabelle often thought about the events of that day. The way Isabelle's life changed so remarkably within a span of a few hours altered more than her general philosophy of life. It changed her. It fostered a tolerance in her for views and ideas she didn't necessarily understand. Isabelle wrote a book about that day – *The Kindness Project* – a book that made her a lot of money. And while the financial resources were a much appreciated windfall, Isabelle's greatest transformation took place far deeper than in her bank account.

"Did you squeeze it yourself?" Isabelle asked about the orange juice.

"I have a juicer, but yes, the oranges were freshly-squeezed this morning," Harriet proudly shared.

Isabelle rarely drank fruit juices, but Harriet's orange juice was sugar-worthy. It was perfectly sweet and pulpy. Isabelle was sure that if there was a heaven, and orange juice in that heaven, this is how it would taste. "Harriet, I don't normally drink fruit juice but that's to die for."

"Well, I'd like to take the credit, but you have to start with sweet oranges to get sweet orange juice," Harriet said.

"Cheers, to a weekend to remember," Isabelle lifted her glass and motioned to Harriet to meet her half way for a toast.

"Cheers!" Hope said.

"Wow!" Isabelle was always amazed at the things her three-year-old picked up on. "Yes, cheers. Very good little one,"

Isabelle said.

"Cheers! Cheers! Cheers!" Hope said, responding to the praise she received from her mom. This made both Isabelle and Harriet laugh.

"I don't know what happens to her in this house, but she's s such a good little eater here," Isabelle observed. "Normally, we have more cereal on the floor and the table than on her plate and in her mouth," Isabelle said, appreciating the effect Harriet somehow had on the child.

"The key is to set proper expectations," Harriet said. "She knows that to be a good girl, we don't throw our food on the floor here. That would never be acceptable."

"Whatever works, Harriet. You know that's my motto," Isabelle said.

Isabelle's phone rang. As she reached for her phone, Harriet spoke up, "Can't it wait a few minutes until we're finished with breakfast?"

Normally, Isabelle would cite her right as an adult to make her own decisions, but not today. Today, they were enjoying such a lovely breakfast. Harriet had outdone herself with perfectly crisp bacon, infused with maple syrup, and served with fresh gluten-free sourdough bread, that Harriet had ordered special from Jenny Mae's Bakery in Yakima, just for Isabelle. The eggs were sunny-side-up with a runny yolk. It was as perfect of a breakfast as Isabelle could ever remember enjoying.

By this time in her life, Isabelle could appreciate the value of sometimes just living in the moment. Besides, when she glanced over at the caller, she could see it was Zach, and she didn't want to take his call with Harriet around. Ten minutes later, just as they were finishing, the phone rang again.

It was an unfamiliar number on her Hushed line. Probably a local contractor. Oh, or maybe the tire shop. She took the call.

"This is Isabelle." There was a pause while she listened. "Oh, hi, Owen. Yes, we're just finishing breakfast. I thought I would walk over to the shop in a few minutes but I should probably call them first," Isabelle said. Harriet could only hear her side of the conversation. "Oh, wow. Thank you. That's so nice of you." Owen had already called the shop and was phoning to let Isabelle know her car was ready for pick-up and he'd be happy to swing by to give her a ride. "No, I think I'm going to walk. I need the steps. But thank you. For everything. You saved the night last night. I don't know what Hope and I would have done if you hadn't come along. I'll see you around, I'm sure." Isabelle hung up the phone.

"You could have called me," Harriet said.

"To be fair, I probably would have since I didn't know you lived so close to the tire shop. But it was still nice of him to help us out that way," Isabelle said.

"How do you know this man exactly?" Harriet asked.

This had been such a perfect morning, aside from the cockerel of course. There was no point in lying. She'd have to remember it and try to make sense of it. And she didn't want to lie to Harriet anyway. "I met him in Maui. He had a Ducks hat on and I thought he was from Oregon. We chatted at Bad Ass coffee by the farmer's market and I honestly didn't expect to see him again until he showed up last night on the interstate," Isabelle said. There is was. Nothing to hide.

"You didn't know him when you accepted a ride from him last night, with Hope in the car?" Harriet questioned.

"I wouldn't have gotten in his truck if I hadn't recognized him from Hawaii. It's not like he was a stranger," Isabelle said. She left out the part about talking to him for an hour after surfing in Hawaii, so she could somewhat understand Harriet's trepidation.

"Well, you were very lucky. Sorta stupid but very lucky,"

Harriet said.

"Turns out he's a nice guy who was willing to help someone he didn't know. I respect that," Isabelle said.

Harriet didn't totally approve but she didn't fight Isabelle on the matter either. The fact was, it was over now and an argument wouldn't have changed the outcome.

"Do you mind watching Hope while I walk over to the tire shop and pick up my car?" Isabelle asked her aunt.

"I already said I'd be happy to," Harriet said. Isabelle was glad she had at least mostly come clean about Owen. She had too much going on to try to create and remember any fictitious stories beyond her latest novel she was writing.

"Thanks!" Isabelle said, kissing her aunt on the cheek as she grabbed her jacket, purse and phone before hurrying out the door. "Bye Hope. I'll be back soon," she called out.

Isabelle enjoyed the short walk to the tire shop. It was a warm, sunny fall morning and the maple trees were just starting to show bits of color on their leaves. She walked past a part of the university campus, and noted her surprise at seeing so many cars in the student parking lot for a Saturday. *I guess it's been a while since I did the whole college thing. I probably studied on Saturdays. Been so long I don't remember.*

Suddenly, it dawned on her that it had been nearly four years – in fact, four years next month – since Harriet had suffered the stroke and been a patient at Providence Portland. She felt as if the last four years had passed so quickly, and simultaneously, that they had been long and hard-fought. A lot had happened in those four years. *How could so much be the same and so much be completely different?* Isabelle felt a chill move through her as she thought about how quickly her life changed.

When she arrived at the tire shop, she spotted a truck that looked like Owen's. *I don't know about this guy. He's nice enough but why does he keep showing up?* She took a deep breath and knew she needed to be nice when she saw him. She had offered to buy him a cup of coffee, after all, and maybe he had showed up to collect on her promise.

Isabelle introduced herself to the counter staff, and thanked them for fitting her in. "Owen called and said you were a friend of his and a friend of his is a friend of ours," the weekend manager, Vince, said.

"Well, that was really nice," she said. "I saw his truck out front. Is he here?"

"Oh he's not here today. He's a volunteer firefighter on Saturdays. You can find him down at the station, unless there's a fire. Then he's on the front lines," said Vince.

Of course. He's a local hero. And I was just assuming he was a pervert who's been stalking me. "That's incredible," Isabelle said. "I thought he was a professor."

"That's his day job. But this is fire country, between here and Cle Elum Those of us who call Ellensburg home are ready at any moment to respond when a fire breaks out," he said.

"That's very neighborly."

"The good news is that we were able to patch your tire and you have enough tread to last at least another five thousand miles," Vince said, changing the subject.

"Thank you," she said. "How much do I owe you?"

"Not a dime, ma'am. Consider this a favor on behalf of a friend. Just pay it forward, preferably here in town," he said.

"I will find a way to do that," she said, as she put her hand out to reach for her car keys.

As she walked away, Isabelle stopped and turned back to look at the tire shop. *Maybe Ellensburg's not so bad.*

CHAPTER 5

When Isabelle arrived back at Harriet's, she found three construction vans in the driveway. *Oh this is not good. Zach isn't going to take this well.* She got out of her car and stood and gazed at the house. She snapped a photo and texted it to him, followed by a brief message: *Guess we're a week late! She seemed pretty determined to do what she wanted when I talked to her and now we know she wasn't bluffing.*

He immediately fired a message back: *Thx for trying.*

That was easy. She smiled. *Let's hope Zach doesn't find out I never confronted Harriet about her spending. Like she would have taken that well from me anyway!* Isabelle shrugged, tucked her purse under her arm and walked inside.

She walked in on Harriet explaining the changes she envisioned. Harriet was exceptional at elucidating exactly what she wanted. And unlike Zach and Isabelle, the contractors seemed to hang on Harriet's every word. As Isabelle listened and observed, she realized the atrium wasn't on Harriet's priority list at all. From what Isabelle could gather, Harriet seemed to want one of the bedrooms turned into a closet and connected to the master bedroom.

Suddenly, Isabelle felt almost as if she were having an out of body experience, watching the events unfold as someone peering through an open window might. A calm came over her as she clearly saw what was really going on. Harriet had found a way to search every last inch of Joy's house, no matter what it cost her. If the diary was indeed still there, Harriet would retrieve it or die trying. Isabelle recognized she had no choice but to switch sides. She could no longer do her brother's dirty work. This wasn't about construction or a house at all. Of course it didn't matter to Harriet what this renovation cost. This was Harriet's final quest to connect with the one person she loved most in this life, and she was willing to spend her last dime to do it.

When Isabelle walked into the kitchen, she noticed a pretty fall bouquet of yellow and orange mums. She appreciated fresh-cut flowers and mentioned them to Harriet as she and her construction entourage passed through the room. "They came for you dear. Your friend Owen sent them," she said as if it were no big deal that she read the card.

"They're not for you from your neighbor as gratitude for listening to that teenage cock of hers crow?" Isabelle asked in jest. Harriet did not find this funny in front of her guests, and she shot Isabelle a motherly look to let her know.

Isabelle picked up the card: *Meet me at Brix tonight at six. You'll love their gluten-free pizza. Owen.*

Isabelle was equally drawn to and frustrated by Owen's unmistakable masculinity. He took control, and she didn't know what to make of his confident style. For more than ten years, Arnie let her call the shots, even if it was reluctantly. She had no experience with someone like Owen, strong-minded and yet ever the gentleman. He let her know early that a relationship with him – even a friendship – would require submission. A part of her wanted to call him and thank him for the flowers, and then tell him in no uncertain terms that she already had plans, if for no other reason than to test his limits. But she didn't have plans and she secretly liked that he took charge. His influence brought out her dormant femininity in a strange way she didn't fully understand, and she liked it.

At least he's a hero. I guess he's entitled to call a few shots, she rationalized. Isabelle felt giddy in anticipation of dinner at the wine bar with the renaissance man who always seemed to show up just when she needed help.

Her phone alerted her of a text message. She looked down and saw it was her brother. She had been avoiding his calls. *Call me.* The same style that seemed sexy from Owen felt oppressive from her brother. She didn't want Harriet to overhear their conversation so she stepped outside.

"What's up?" Isabelle asked when Zach answered the phone. She listened to him ramble on about the frivolous atrium before she jumped in. "I don't think she's focused on an atrium right now," Isabelle said. "Zach, stop. From what I overheard, I think she needs some basic help with a closet and maybe some painting. You know Harriet. She's probably trying to shine a little handyman work on the husband of someone at her church. I think we should back off." And just like that, Isabelle had not only changed sides but was advocating for Harriet.

Owen would not have been drawn to Harriet. Despite her conservative views, Harriet suffered no fools, of any gender, that even tried to tell her what to do. No man would dare send Harriet flowers and tell her to show up at six.

Isabelle was not like Harriet in this way. Despite her progressive worldly views, Isabelle longed to meet a man who made her feel cared for. While still getting to know Owen, she already knew she appreciated his masculinity. As much as Isabelle bickered with Zach over the years, she often wished Arnie would have taken charge more often and been more like her brother in this way.

As she looked at Harriet, and thought about Zach, a small part of Isabelle relished even the thought of a showdown between Harriet and her brother. Zach frequently worked behind the scenes, making suggestions and sending Isabelle to do his bidding. Isabelle imagined a Pay-Per-View special of Harriet and Zach in a ring, each boxing the air. She laughed aloud. *Who would win?* She smiled thinking what a *tour de jeu* that would be. *Harriet would totally win!* It was a fun escape, but Isabelle couldn't focus on that now. She had an outfit to pick out.

Just as Isabelle started walking toward the guestroom, she stopped cold in her tracks, as she became astutely aware of a pattern. The hall wall was covered in framed photos, of her parents, Zach and her from before the accident. *Were these always here?*

Looking at the photos brought back so many memories of who she was as a child, decades ago. The photos captured a time when life was carefree. From the time Zach and she were kids, they teased each other relentlessly. Even as a child, he was so quick-witted that even as a tot, she learned to think of zingers and comebacks long before she ever needed them.

What seemed like a random question occurred to her. *When does banter morph into meanness?* She and Zach were not on opposite sides. It was Zach who made it possible for her to keep her house before her book became a best-seller. And she and Harriet were not opponents either. Harriet had done more for Isabelle than she could ever repay.

Isabelle instantly felt regret over so many of her thoughts and words over the last four years. Her moods had been so erratic and her temper sometimes harsh. There were times she was sad and miserable and times when her wiser, confident and even charitable self prevailed. And in that moment, Isabelle even felt a twinge of guilt for the snarky thoughts that crossed her mind but never left her lips.

Maturity came with a filter and a promise that thinking something was one thing and saying it, quite another. She couldn't imagine releasing the pleasure of her thought bubbles. It was her private thoughts that kept her safe, sane and entertained.

On her way back to the guestroom, she peeked in on Hope, who had fallen asleep on the floor, bent over her dolls. Isabelle quietly tip-toed into the room and reached down to pick up her little girl. She held her in her arms and rocked her before gently laying her down on the twin bed. She leaned down and kissed her forehead and then stopped fighting the urge to snuggle next to her and breathe in her fresh skin. Isabelle laid down beside her toddler and curled her body like a spoon around her child. Hope was small for her age. She had Arnie's delicate build.

Isabelle thought back to what a dark place her life had been in less than two years before. She never could have imagined being so happy and finally feeling successful. Not to mention, she had love on the horizon with potentially two men. How would she decide between the foreign exchange student from her past, and the professor-turned-volunteer firefighter who pushed her buttons in all the right places?

Isabelle reveled in this unexpected place she found herself. She knew life came with struggles, and so long as she had breath she could count on new trials not yet on the horizon. But for this one moment, spooning her little girl, and thinking about how truly amazing her life felt, all she could offer up was gratitude.

◆ ◆ ◆

As Isabelle looked at the clothes she brought from Portland, none of them were especially date-worthy. Twenty-four hours before neither the possibility of Owen nor Masingho loomed on the horizon. She was pretty sure Saturday night would have been spent watching The History Channel or *Dateline* with Harriet. Isabelle loved documentaries and news magazine shows. But to be fair, she didn't dress up for dinner in with her aunt.

She scrunched her nose as she considered her options for date night attire. *I may need to run downtown and pick up something new.* She nodded, pleased with herself for thinking of that. This was all new territory. Isabelle hadn't been on a date since Arnie died – unless she counted coffee with Owen in Maui. *So in a way, this may be our second date. I hope he kisses me.*

◆ ◆ ◆

When Isabelle arrived at the wine bar with the brick walls and big windows, Owen was already there, and had ordered her a glass of merlot. "How did you know I prefer red?" she asked.

"Just a hunch. I would have replaced it if you wanted something else," Owen said. He had a brilliant smile. "You look nice," he said.

"Thank you." Isabelle blushed. *Maybe this hero isn't so bad after all.* "So what's your favorite kind of pizza?" she asked, changing the subject.

"I have a few. Canadian bacon and pineapple or a nice hearty sausage and veggie combo. As long as it has fresh sliced tomatoes on the top, I'm happy."

"A man who's easy to please. That's always a good start." Isabelle flirted.

After the server took their order Isabelle had so many questions for the handsome man with warm brown eyes, who was quickly growing on her. "So how did you decide to be a volunteer firefighter in your spare time?

"I'm a water fanatic," he answered, setting her up to continue asking questions.

"A water fanatic? So the lifeguarding spots at the local public pool were filled?"

"Nice. But no." He paused for effect, and it worked because she leaned in. "My specialty is environmental microbiology, and here in Central Washington, nothing impacts us more than water. Water reservoirs, water levels, melting water, water for the fish, water for the farmers. And of course water to fight fires. As a firefighter, I'm able to work on the fire line and observe first-hand the changes to our ecosystem."

Wow! He sounds really smart. "So you do it for research basically?" Isabelle asked.

"Sure, but it's more than that. We're all neighbors here. A fire can have far-reaching implications to the families directly involved, as well as livestock, local businesses and the whole region."

"Plus it makes you sound like a hero," Isabelle teased.

"Sound like a hero? I am a bona fide, card-carrying hero." Owen smiled, speaking slowly to intentionally tease her. Owen reached for his wallet as if there was really a card for such.

"It's why I agreed to go out with you," Isabelle said with a wink, just as the server was arriving with their dinner salads. *You know. Maybe I was wrong about him in Maui. I think I like this one. Maybe a lot.*

"Two honey mustards on the side," the server said as she set down the salads. "Can I get you anything else before your pizza arrives?"

"This is great," Owen said.

"I don't remember ordering a salad," Isabelle said.

"I took the liberty of ordering for us. I hope that's okay," Owen said. "Honey mustard, right?"

"Do you always make decisions for the women in your life?" Isabelle asked in a joking but also challenging tone. She wasn't about to let him know she liked him doing this, yet.

"It's gluten-free, and it's their house. Try it. It's good." Owen said.

Isabelle reached down and dipped her fork in the dressing cup and then into the spring mix. "This is pretty terrific." Isabelle caved. "I'm going to give you this round, hero."

This made Owen laugh. He reached over and brushed her hand with his. He clearly enjoyed that she called him "Hero."

"What other surprises do you have for me tonight?" she asked, just as their pizza was being delivered.

"You like the dressing, wait until you bite into the pizza," Owen said with a wink.

Who is this man? Owen dished up two slices on a plate for Isabelle and two slices for himself. "Thank you," Isabelle said as she picked up her fork to take a bite.

"Oh man, don't be such a city girl. It's pizza. Pick it up," Owen commanded.

Isabelle was relieved. "I was hoping you'd say that. But I didn't want to be rude and eat with my hands on a first date and all."

"When we were having coffee in Maui, something about you seemed incredibly familiar," Owen said. "I felt like I knew you even though we just met."

"I thought the same thing," Isabelle said.

Owen debated telling Isabelle that he realized the connection back in Maui, but he sensed she might bust his chops for not addressing it at the time. All he knew was that he needed to come clean about the ring and the fact that she was never a stranger to him. "You are very beautiful," he said, hoping those words would buy him enough time to know which direction to take.

It worked. She blushed, smiled and nervously glanced

down at her salad before looking back up and locking eyes with him. "Thank you," she replied, confidently.

The time had come. He had to go for it. He knew it was now or never. "So when I dropped you off at Harriet's, after your flat tire last night – although the house and yard look radically different – I realized who you are," Owen said.

This got Isabelle's attention. "I lived there as a kid," she said.

"I know. I was in your brother Zach's class, up until fifth grade," Owen said.

All the color washed out of Isabelle's face. *Please don't bring up the accident.* She completely changed the subject to her modern day situation with her brother. "Oh, he's been driving me crazy all week with his bossy calls. Older brothers can be seriously bossy, especially Zach. Do you have siblings?" Isabelle rambled hoping to change the subject to Owen's family.

"No biological siblings. Lots of friends, an honorary nephew, and a few cousins throughout Washington and Oregon," Owen said. *Yes! It worked.* This pleased Isabelle and the smile returned to her face. "You didn't tell me your family moved to Oregon," Owen said.

"I didn't think so," Isabelle said.

"I guess my mind filled that in, subconsciously remembering the accident," Owen said.

And there it is. Out there. Now he will want to talk about it, and tell me how sorry he is, like that will somehow make a difference. And I'll say it's fine and of course it will be awkward.

"You picked the perfect place. The pizza here is fantastic. So you're a professor, a volunteer firefighter and a closet foodie. Anything else I need to know?" Isabelle asked playfully.

Owen was dying to tell her about the ring. Once he could get that off his chest, he was sure his blood pressure would instantly return to normal. *Well maybe not instantly – she is gorgeous*, he thought.

Just as she finished her questions, and took a sumptuous bite, another couple walked up to their table. "Hey Owen, how are ya? Where's Jill tonight?" the man asked. Isabelle could tell Owen was immediately and visibly uncomfortable.

Jill? Who's Jill? Isabelle was prone to a wandering mind and jealous inclinations when she lacked enough information to feel secure.

"Working – you know how busy she is." Owen quickly answered and seemed to turn his shoulders away from them as if to discourage a long conversation. *Something is not right here.*

"Who's Jill?" Isabelle finally asked the question her mind had been fussing about.

Owen slid his hand into his front pocket – the pocket containing Arnie's ring. "She's a colleague. More of a friend. We're working on a water project together. She's a patent attorney," Owen answered.

"Oh, I thought you guys lived together?" The woman questioned Owen. But before he could answer, she turned and introduced herself to Isabelle. "Hi, I'm Amy. What's your connection to Owen?" the woman asked pointedly, shoving her hand into Isabelle's space for an intrusive handshake. *Isabelle felt panicked. She suddenly wasn't sure how to answer. She certainly didn't want any more pizza, or wine for that matter.*

"I met Owen surfing in Maui and he helped me with a flat tire last night," Isabelle said. Suddenly, Isabelle realized she may have misread this entire situation. *Maybe this isn't a date?* She wasn't really sure what to think in light of these unexpected visitors.

"Awe, good ol' Owen, always the knight in shining armor," Amy teased, slapping his shoulder awkwardly. "Well it was nice to meet you, Isabelle. Owen, tell Jill we said hi."

He inhaled deeply and nodded. The color had drained from his face by the time they walked away.

"Were you going to mention you had a live-in girlfriend at some point on our date, or is this not a date?" Isabelle was confused. She could have tried to hide it but she didn't see the value in that. *I do not need some small-town douche bag adding me to his clearly busy dance card. I live in Portland where there are plenty of men. Plenty!*

"She's not my girlfriend," Owen said, emphatically, but without further explanation.

"I'm not a cheater and I'm not really interested in getting involved with one either," Isabelle said as she stood up and reached for her purse. "Is there anything else you've neglected to tell me or is this it?"

Arnie's ring in his pocket was poking him. The desire to come clean created an expression of constipation on his face. He desperately wanted to tell her about the ring – needed to tell her, but he just didn't see that this was the time. "No," he said, disappointed with himself for letting the moment to return Isabelle's cherished ring pass. Despite his discomfort, he forced himself to explain. "Please don't leave."

"Why should I stay?" she asked, giving him one more chance. She really liked him.

"You don't understand. Jill and I are working on a patent for a technology that could transform water access for the entire region. This is so much bigger than one or two people," Owen said.

Isabelle sat back down. "Oh, I get it. So you're business partners and roommates? Why didn't you just say that?"

"Well, yes." Owen was side-stepping the discussion. Isabelle realized this and didn't like his hesitancy in responding.

She wasn't going to beat around the bush. "Are you sleeping with her?"

Owen sighed. "We're not dating. I'm trying to help humanity. I'm trying to save the water. She's helping with that," he said. *You didn't answer my question, Owen.*

"I'll take that as a yes. Well, good luck with that. I don't date cheaters. Thanks for your help with my tire but don't call me again," Isabelle said as she stood back up and stormed out of the restaurant.

Isabelle felt mostly angry, mixed with a touch of sadness and disappointment as she walked the half a block to her car. *Some hero. I really liked you. Boy, do you have this town fooled.* She refused to cry. Mascara smudges would likely draw questions from Harriet, and she didn't want to talk about it. She wanted to put the professor in her rearview mirror. *I can't wait to return to Portland tomorrow. I knew he was a jerk when I met him in Honokawai, posing as a Duck. You're going to save humanity, alright, in your own dumb fantasy. Stupid professor.*

◆ ◆ ◆

"Do you really think this is a good idea? I mean, do you even know anything about him?" Zach questioned his sister in the manner Isabelle was used to from Harriet.

"Relax. I'm going to Seattle for a book signing. We're going to meet for dinner. That's all. I'm not in love with him. I'm not moving to Portugal. I'm having dinner with an old friend." Zach knew his sister and he knew Masingho was hardly an old friend.

Isabelle also knew dinner with Masingho was a lot more significant than she was letting on to her brother. It was either a fresh start or closure with a lost love. And given her disastrous dinner with Owen, she was open to just about anything with Masingho that would take her mind off the professor. Isabelle saw no point in telling Zach about Owen, even though they had been classmates. She assumed it would only lead to more questions and Zach drawing more conclusions, and she didn't want to go down that road.

The last four years, since losing Arnie, had changed Isabelle's view about the supernatural. She had started to believe in things that up until that time she would have merely shrugged off. While she still didn't consider herself fundamentally religious, she warmly embraced that her connection to God had mysteriously become exceedingly real. Instead of making her bitter, the hardships of the previous years tenderized her heart and strengthened her connection to what mattered most in her life today.

And then something else dawned on her. Half of her silent conversations in her head, which she always considered *talking to herself*, were actually micro-prayers, inwardly trusting that someone bigger would somehow light her way. *Oh Lord, I have loved this man so long. Please give him a great love for me or take away my love and connection to him.*

CHAPTER 6

At the bookstore, Isabelle looked up and saw the man who had remained young in her mind. Seeing him now with gray in his beard and the same natural highlights depicting his age throughout his curls was like looking at a dream for her. It didn't feel completely real. She looked up from the pile of books and the line of readers waiting for her autograph. It was as if time stood still as she inhaled slowly a lungful of air. At first she forced herself to smile, barely tipping the edges of her mouth up, lips pressed together. But when he smiled back, she came alive inside. A large grin spread across her face and her eyes twinkled.

Laurie, the bookstore manager, standing beside Isabelle, unexpectedly got caught between the former lovers. She glanced at Masingho and then at Isabelle. "You're flushed," she blurted out, then tried to compensate for her bold observance by covering her mouth after the fact.

Isabelle was shocked to be experiencing a physical re-action. She intentionally grabbed a hold of herself. Isabelle's eyes softened as a wave of peace flowed over her. The magnetic pull between them was no longer sewn together with expect-ations. *So this is what forgiveness feels like.*

After the signing, Isabelle found Masingho in the back of the bookstore, browsing shelves of book titles. She could see the boy she once loved in his eyes, despite the creases time left at the corners. She held out her arms to welcome a hug. "I'm a hugger," she said, titling her head to the side and smiling. He sunk into her.

"I always loved that about you," he said.

"I'm glad you could come," she said. "I hoped you would."

"Isabella, you look most beautiful. Your pictures really don't do you justice," he said.

Isabelle blushed. "Thank you. You look the same."

"Not to be confused with beautiful," he said, winking playfully. That made her laugh, but she didn't correct him. Masingho had never been classically handsome, even in his youth. Nonetheless, she was wildly attracted to him from the moment they met.

"Shall we grab coffee before dinner," Masingho observed.

He bought her coffee at a small cupcake shop, and the pair walked arm in arm, much the way they had twenty years before. "I forgive you," she stated unprovoked. This made him noticeably uncomfortable.

"I'm not a good man. I haven't made the best choices in life. But I regret hurting you," Masingho said. He stopped and faced her, looking her square in the eyes. "If I could change one thing about my life, I would change that."

She inhaled slowly and breathed all the air out of her lungs before responding. She turned forward and took his arm so they could continue walking, not facing each other. "Thank you," she said. *His apology felt like a cool mist on a hot day. She was eager for more. She was eager to hear how knowing her had ultimately made him a better man.* She smiled, trying desperately not to wrinkle her face, but failing as tears filled her eyes. Her tongue nervously licked her bottom lip as a small trickle of tears slipped over her lower lids.

The truth was, he had hurt her – deeply. She wondered for years why he never came back, and never called to let her know or say goodbye. At times, she wondered if he was even alive, believing he would certainly reach out to her if only he could. She talked to him in her sleep, hoping somehow to make a telepathic connection. But that connection never took place. It was always as if an imaginary wall separated them. Finally, after she let him go the last time, he came back. *What is it that he must want now? A second chance?* In some ways, this was everything she had hoped and even prayed for so many times. In other ways, it was as if a glorious feast was prepared and set before her, only it was just a picture or an image in a mirror. As much as she could smell it and imagine tasting its perfection, it was a mirage.

Masingho wanted to walk away. He appeared visibly uncomfortable. The look on his face spoke volumes. He regretted coming. He clenched his teeth. This is the scene he would have moved mountains to avoid. Instead, she kept her arm wrapped around his and tipped her head onto the shoulder of his five-foot-eight frame.

A part of Isabelle wanted to let him off the hook – to change the subject. But she knew in that moment they would either be together forever, or this would be the last time she would ever see him. And if that was the case, she needed to finish the chapter in her mind so she could truly move forward. Even knowing these options, she wasn't ready to make a choice. Not yet. In that exact moment, she held tightly to the hope that his love for her matched the torch she had carried so long for him.

"I admire you," she said.

"You shouldn't," he quickly retorted. "I was a terrible husband and I'm barely adequate as a dad. You deserve better."

"I believe that," she said, half laughing. For years, Isabelle had fantasized about this reunion. But never once did she imagine it playing out this way.

Air escaped his lungs with such swiftness it forced him to cough.

She continued. "I admire that on some level you had to have known or feared that this could happen and you still had the courage to come. So why did you come?" Isabelle remembered her prayer, and for the first time, she started to worry that Masingho didn't truly love her the way she loved him.

"I thought you'd be angry with me. I thought you would hate me," he said. "But I figured if I was right, you'd refuse to see me. And if I was wrong, we'd end up in bed."

Isabelle laughed. "Not a chance on the second one."

"Can't blame a guy for trying," he shrugged.

"I've loved you. I've hated you too over the years. I've imagined this story playing out a dozen different ways. And I've made peace with letting you go," she said.

"I've only ever loved you," he said. "I pushed you away because I was terrified of failing you, of making you hate me, of loving you and not having you love me back."

On some level, these were the words Isabelle longed to hear; and yet, they didn't feel genuine. They were just words strung together to create a great pick-up line. Masingho's words failed to match his body language or the energy between them.

"Do you remember what you said to me the last night we were together?" Isabelle asked.

"I do. It haunts me. I'm sorry. I wish I could take back those words. If only life had a reset button. I am sorry and I hope that's enough," he looked down at his shoes when he whispered that to her.

"Do you know why I forgave you?" Isabelle asked.

"Why?" He asked, shaking his head.

"For a long time I didn't. I was in a marriage to a man who

I loved, and who truly loved me. But he never lived up to my fantasies of you. For a decade, my life was with him, but my heart was with you – not you, really, but who I built you up to be in my mind," she said.

Masingho took his arm out of hers and wrapped it around her shoulder and drew her into himself. "Oh Isabella, I'm so sorry," he said, shaking his head back and forth in regret.

"We were going through a divorce when he died. Our daughter, Grace, wanted us back together and we were trying so hard for her to make things work. We got back together for one night. We made love and he left to get a change of clothes for an early morning meeting. He was gone the longest time, and then he called. Only it wasn't him. It was a paramedic, urging me to drop whatever I was doing to go to the hospital."

"That sounds horrific."

"It was. Even worse, it took losing Arnie to discover how much I also loved him – in a very different way than I loved you." Isabelle paused to give Masingho a chance to jump in – and he did.

"Was this a mistake? Me coming?" Masingho asked.

"Heavens no. I needed you to come. I needed to walk arm-in-arm with you again and reconnect with you as a real person so I could release the fantasy of you from my mind. Your coming was the greatest gift you've ever given me – other than, I suppose, walking away when we were young."

"Hmm," Masingho grunted.

"I dated Arnie because he was everything you weren't and he took my mind off of you. If you hadn't said what you did, if you hadn't destroyed me, carved out my heart and left a gaping hole no amount of time could ever heal, I wouldn't have been so desperate to fill that void with him. And I would have missed out on sweet Hope. She is such a good toddler. And Grace. Wow,

Grace. She's a feisty preteen now, but truth be told, she's the most redeeming achievement of my life. Despite the fact that she hates me right now."

"Don't all teenagers hate their parents?" Masingho asked, half in jest. Isabelle wanted to respond. *I didn't. My parents were dead when I was a teenager. I would have given anything to have them, even for one day. How could you forget that?* But she didn't share this. Not with Masingho. Not now. There was no point.

"Hope is a happy baby. I don't ever remember being that happy as a child. I swear she giggles more than anyone I've ever known. She takes after her dad in that way. He was so fun. Too fun sometimes. I wanted him to be more serious, but fun was probably what I really needed," she said.

"I'm truly sorry," he said. "I'm sorry I carved out your heart. You're the last person I would have wanted to do that to."

"I know. I know that because you showed up. You didn't just send an instant message or flowers with a note tucked inside. You showed up. It couldn't have been easy for you. But you did and I genuinely honor that." The two of them strolled the Magnolia waterfront outside of Maggie's, stopping to sit on the wooden benches and look out at the boats? "Will you honestly answer a lingering question in my mind?" Isabelle asked.

He paused uncomfortably. "Men hate questions like this, just so you know. But I'll try," Masingho said.

She didn't care that he was uncomfortable. He had made her uncomfortable for years – decades even. She knew where they stood at this point and she wanted closure. She needed closure. "Why are you here? Why did you contact me? Why did you come?" Isabelle asked.

"My company is opening an office in Seattle. I'm going to be here at least once a month. I don't want to tie you down with a commitment, but if you'd agree, I'd like to see you when I'm in town – a second chance of sorts," Masingho offered.

"I'm unclear what you are offering. You want to date me long-distance when you are in town?" Isabelle asked.

"I think about our time together in college and later in San Francisco. Wouldn't you like to have that again? We could meet for weekends in Paris or Sao Paulo. I can give you a life of adventure and you could write. Let me spoil you, Isabella. Let me give you everything you've ever wanted." Masingho laid out a proposal he was sure she couldn't decline.

Isabelle was silent for the longest time. *He has no clue who I am or what I want.*

"What are you thinking? Tell me what you're thinking? Are you considering my offer?" Masingho asked excitedly.

"You've known me since we were kids. How could you possibly think I would settle for being anyone's mistress or in-town girl? How could you even entertain that thought?" Isabelle was genuinely crushed.

"I suppose it's a taboo way of putting things for Americans but imagine a life of love without the confines of monogamy and commitment. I can offer you all the upside without any of the ties that bind." Masingho wasn't trying to be a jerk. He simply lived life through a different lens.

Isabelle was visibly upset. "I can't believe," she paused, "I can't believe I idealized you for one single day. I can't believe I spent nights wishing you were here and days wondering what might have been. Of everything I wondered and considered about a life with you in a parallel universe, I never once imagined you would come back and offer me trips and dinner for sex," Isabelle said. "That's all you ever wanted."

"Don't be angry. Don't do this," Masingho pleaded.

"I'm not angry." And suddenly she wasn't. A strange calm came over her body and her voice. The answer to her prayer was occurring in real time. Every ounce of love she ever felt for Masingho was melting away. "Every time Arnie let me down, I im-agined a perfect life with you," Isabelle explained.

"We can have that. That's exactly what I am offering you, Isabella. You an write by day and we can make love by the light of the moon at night."

"At our age? We're in our mid-forties, and I'm a mother of two. That's a college-age fantasy." Isabelle laid it out.

"Just on weekends, Isabella. The rest of the time you can live your life doing whatever else pleases you." Masingho did not hear her.

"Stop calling me Isabella. My name is Isabelle." Isabelle was rarely so sharp in her responses, but despite her tone, she wasn't angry. She was hurt. She felt crushed beyond what she imagined was possible.

"I can see it was a mistake for me to reach out to you," Masingho said.

"I guess in some weird horrible way this was probably a gift. My fantasies of you could have tainted relationships the rest of my life. It's better I finally know the truth about you. Did you know you were my first love?" She paused as tears trickled down her face. "And it was an amazing love, at least for me. We were young, poor, and clearly free to exercise poor judgment."

"How can you blame me for wanting to recreate that?" Masingho asked.

Because we're not young, poor and inexperienced anymore. Isabelle thought this but what came out of her mouth was more diplomatic. Isabelle sighed. "I don't blame you. We're differ-ent people. I want a relationship with someone I can count on through all the seasons of life. Because let me tell you, I've been through a lot the past four years. And great sex is awesome, but it doesn't begin to compare to the security of feeling safe. I need a man who makes me feel safe. And you're never going to be that man."

"Maybe I could be?" Masingho suggested.

"I'm done settling, Masingho. I deserve more. I want to build a life with someone who isn't afraid to lead and respects my need to follow."

"This is good. I like to take charge," Masingho said.

"I don't judge you. I just don't want what you have to offer. I'm sorry." Isabelle stared up at the sky as if she could unzip the clouds and climb up and out of this scenario.

"What if you think about it over dinner?" Masingho requested.

"I don't want dinner. Not with you."

"Let me buy you dinner. You can save your money for your children," he said.

This unleashed a hot button. She had been poor for years after Arnie – so poor she did struggle to feed her children. But she wasn't anymore and she didn't want or need anyone's pity, let alone his. "I'm a best-selling author, Masingho. I don't need anyone to buy me dinner." Her tone was snobbish, which was not intended, and somehow he understood and sidestepped this.

Although, he was completely broadsided by Isabelle's lack of interest in any part of his offer. "So where do we go from here?" he asked.

Normally Isabelle would have hated someone forcing her to make a decision like that. She never dreamed she'd be the one to shut the door completely on the man she fantasized about for decades. This was a decision Isabelle had thought about a hundred different times and ways, but never in this way. *Wow! When God closes a door He really closes a door.*

"A part of me will always love you – or at least the fantasy of you in my mind. But I want something completely different than what you want and need right now – and maybe ever. I'm a mom, a sister, and a daughter to Harriet, who despite what she thinks, really does need me now," she said, as an auspicious look of wisdom washed across her face.

"I promised you wine and dinner. At least let me pull a chair out for you and order your favorite dessert. I know you have to eat." Masingho tried his best to keep the door open.

"You've given me so much more than dinner, and I seriously thank you," she said. She gently slid her hand out of his and started to slowly step backward, moving away from him."

"So is this goodbye?" he asked.

"If I could write our ending, we would be friends. I would watch your daughter grow up and you would watch mine, even from the distance of Facebook," she offered. "But I'm not sure that would be good for either of us. And I can't imagine the right man for me – whoever and wherever he is – being okay with you hanging around given our history."

"Well, if he exists, he's a lucky man," Masingho said.

"After Arnie died, I made a conscious decision to celebrate each day as it presented, and live for tomorrow – not for a past that I couldn't change. I wasn't always good at that. There were some dark years. But by the grace of God, I survived, and I learned to look for the light," Isabelle said.

"That's very new age of you," Masingho joked.

"You're not the man I knew twenty years ago. And to be fair, I'm not that girl. But I wish you well always. I want only the best for you. Just not with me." Light and compassion replaced any judgment she felt minutes before.

Masingho walked toward her, pulled her close, and leaned in, foreheads touching. "You're wrong about something. You are still the girl I knew and loved. What twenty-two-year-old guy wouldn't be terrified by such a fierce butterfly as you?" Masingho was sincere in his compliment. She exhaled as she placed her right palm over her heart as if she were pledging allegiance to a flag.

Isabelle considered kissing him one last time. She wanted to. At first, she had to physically stop herself. Everything about him turned her on. It always did. Their lips were inches apart. She fought the urge exploding inside her on a second-by-second basis.

Suddenly, the desire pulling her in just moments before, melted, like a runny, dripping ice cream cone in one hundred degree weather. *Isabelle!* She silently addressed herself in her own private thoughts. *This has to stop. You have to stop this. A part of you will always love him. But the fantasies, the daydreaming, the running in circles -- it needs to stop here.*

She released the fantasy and regrouped. "Thank you," she said as she wrapped her arms around him and held him close. "For loving me – then – and now." Isabelle paused for a handful of seconds before snapping back to the reality of her current-day commitments. "I should go." She slid her phone out of her pocket and looked at the time.

"I'll see you, online?" he asked the question, rather than making an assumption. She didn't respond.

"Have a safe flight home," she said. As she walked away she turned around and he was still standing there, hands in his jean pockets, watching her walk away. When she turned, he took one hand out, moved his fingers to his lips, and blew her a kiss, the way he did when they were young.

She reached her right hand up, as if to catch it mid-air, as she had done when they were young. Only instead of following through, she simply used her hand to slide her hair behind her ear, before turning back around.

When Isabelle shut her car door, she relaxed into the soft

leather seats and once again exhaled. She laid her head back and smiled without regret. She trusted her instincts. *Thank you. Thank you.* Isabelle started the car, placed her right hand on the gearshift and moved the silver knob to drive. *Goodbye Masingho.*

As Isabelle drove away, she found herself in nearly the same position as she had spent the last four years up until ten days prior. Only now, she was crystal clear on what she wanted in her future. Now could she finally discover the love she had waited for so long.

CHAPTER 7

Tuesday morning, after dropping Grace at school, Isabelle drove to Zach and Amone's house on autopilot. She had put the weekend behind her and looked forward to genuinely reconnecting with Amone while her brother was out of town. Given the tension between Zach and Isabelle over Harriet's unusual investment in the Ellensburg house, driving Amone to her in vitro appointment reminded Isabelle that Zach still trusted her.

Isabelle pulled into the large, circular driveway, turned off her car and unbuckled her seatbelt to get out of the car. Amone was ready and watching for her; she was nearly to the car as Isabelle opened her car door. "Oh, you're here. I was going to ring the bell." Isabelle said as she walked over and gave Amone a hug. It was evident Amone had been crying. "Hey, hey, are you okay? What's going on?" Isabelle asked.

Amone shook her head side-to-side. "It's these hormones. I'll be glad when this is over."

"I know," Isabelle said. *Why did I say that? I have no idea what she's going through.*

Isabelle pulled out of the driveway slowly. "Do you want to stop at Starbucks for some tea?" she asked, pushing her hair behind her ears. Isabelle often played with her hair when she was nervous or didn't know what to say.

"That would be great," Amone said. "Can we just do the drive-through?"

"Of course." Isabelle gave a weak smile. From the time Amone walked into her brother's life, Isabelle had wondered how any woman could be so consistently perfect. It was aggravating to her at times, but recently, Amone was struggling to hold it together and Isabelle was at a loss for how to respond. If it hadn't been for Amone advocating the publishing company where she worked to give Isabelle a contract for her first book, Isabelle would still be working at the insurance job she hated. Amone had been there when she needed her most. Isabelle felt she owed Amone a great deal, beyond truly caring for her as a sister-in-law.

"Can I just talk to you openly?" Amone asked, her normally thin frame puffy and her usual bright eyes encircled in dark rings with drooping skin underneath her lower lids.

Isabelle let Amone talk while she pulled through the drive-through and drove to the IVF clinic. Isabelle appreciated the diversion to focus outside of her own challenges with men and life.

"I'm too old for this. I honestly don't care if we ever get pregnant at this point," Amone started, looking for a response but receiving none. "This IVF process is draining me and making home life next to impossible." Amone paused.

"How so?" Isabelle asked.

"Well there's the hassle of it. You don't just do IVF. IVF becomes your whole focus and everything else revolves around it. And I'm sure you can imagine how your brother responds to that. Zach doesn't like his routines disrupted. He disrupts mine and that's okay, but once he has a plan – which he doesn't always tell me – I'm just supposed to agree and go along with it and be happy. And frankly, it's getting to be too much. I just want to tell him that maybe we should adopt. There are so many kids who need good homes and why are putting ourselves through this? It's exhausting and crazy."

"It does seem like a lot to undergo." Isabelle tried to be supportive.

"You know what's crazy? He didn't even want kids. I wanted them and he wanted to make me happy. But now he's on board and I'm not sure I still am." Amone said.

"On board with having kids or something bigger?" Isabelle hated to ask that question, and feared the answer, but she knew Amone needed her to ask.

Amone started to cry. "I don't know," she whimpered. *Great, I've messed up Harriet's renovation and now I'm going to mess up Amone. Zach is going to kill me!*

"You know what I learned the last few years?" Isabelle asked.

"What?"

"The path of life does not follow our plans. It sounds obvious but it's the complete opposite of the *create the life you want* philosophy we all bought into. Life is what blind-sides us when we're dreaming of what could or should happen. And the only way to really manage it is to either proactively pursue solutions or sidetrack yourself with distractions – and most of those are not positive." Isabelle paused for Amone to jump in, but when she didn't, Isabelle continued. "You have this big, hard, ugly challenge, but you're pursuing a solution. You're getting in vitro. If it doesn't work, then you change course. But you've been through so much, don't you owe it to yourself and your marriage to see it through?" Isabelle asked.

"I guess."

"I took a lot of bad turns. And a lot of bad things happened. You watched me fall apart the last few years and you helped me up. But the worst enemy through all of it was myself.

Because I allowed myself to be victimized by my circumstances for way too long. And I don't say this out of arrogance. I say this because I love you and I'd like to spare you some of the rocks in the road I wish I had stepped around." Isabelle reached over and squeezed Amone's hand.

Amone nodded yes through the tears.

"Do you love my brother?" Isabelle asked.

"I do," Amone said, unenthusiastically. She sniffled and wiped her eyes with her sleeve. "Can we talk about something else? How was your weekend in Ellensburg? Or were you in Seattle? I'm sorry. The days blend into weeks for me."

"Completely disastrous!" Isabelle said, laughing, which made Amone laugh, then cough, then laugh again.

"I can appreciate that," Amone laughed through her tear-stained face. "What happened?"

"Well let's see, in a word – men!" Isabelle said.

"Plural?" Amone asked, interested?

"It's all good," Isabelle said.

"Please distract me from IVF. Tell me what's going on with you." Amone begged.

"Well, I'm struggling with your husband. I can't figure out how to make him hear me. Harriet is pouring money into mom and dad's little yellow house. You should drive up with Zach and see it. She's redone just about everything and he's not pleased with what he calls her little real estate investment. And he's not pleased that I haven't been able to persuade her to stop spending her money this way." Isabelle said.

"Zach is on edge with the IVF. It's not you. You're an easy target. Right now, Harriet's property project is his distraction for what we have going on," Amone said. "So tell me about Harriet's renovation. Zach makes comments here and there but he hasn't told me very much about what's going on," Amone said. "Whenever I ask him questions, he changes the subject."

"Well, Basically Harriet is sinking a ton of money into a property that is very sentimental to her but not a great investment. And Zach's hot under the collar about it. I don't know why he cares so much. It's her money and it's not like he's short on cash," Isabelle said.

"I'm sure he needs to be able to control something." Amone sighed.

"So, I think, Harriet is on a secret mission that she hasn't shared with anyone, including me. But I've kinda pieced it together," Isabelle teased.

"Oh do tell," Amone inquired.

"Well, when we were in Hawaii, Grace had a dream that there was a fire and Harriet had run into the fire to get a book." Isabelle started.

"A house fire?" Amone asked.

"I'm pretty sure." Isabelle said.

"That sounds like a nightmare, especially for a child." Amone reasoned. "Do you think it was a premonition?"

"I bet it was to help us figure out how to help Harriet find what she's searching for," Isabelle said.

"So what do you think the book represents?" Amone asked.

"I kinda think it's an actual book."

"Oooo. Like a diary?" Amone asked.

"That would make sense. It would have to be something that was important enough to run into a fire for. A family Bible. A photo album. A journal. Something she would risk her life for." Isabelle said.

"Have you asked Grace about it?" Amone questioned.

"No. I don't want to upset her."

"That makes sense. So you think Harriet is doing all these renovations in an effort to unearth a lost diary or book." Amone's statement felt like a question to Isabelle.

"All I know is that Harriet is looking for something in that house – something that will get her closer to our mom. And that's why she doesn't care about sinking an insane amount of money into the property. She's financially set. She knows Zach and I are comfortable now. It's not about the money, Amone. Harriet is trying to connect with her sister and somehow that house is involved. I just know it." Isabelle said.

"Sometimes I wish I had married a more sensitive man," Amone said.

Whoa! How am I supposed to respond to that?

"Zach loves you." Isabelle said. "I never thought he would marry. Until you came along. You complement him. You bring out the best in him."

"We were friends first, connected by Winnie. How couldn't I love a man who loved my dog so much, who took such amazing care of her? I loved him as a friend before I ever knew I cared about him romantically. Being around him was as effort-less as breathing. It was like being with myself. It was ridicu-lously awesome." Amone smiled, deep and sincere. "Sometimes I wish we could just be friends again. We were so perfect then. We were great until this whole stupid in vitro thing." Amone stopped talking. Isabelle bit her bottom lip to prevent herself from commenting. "The last couple of years have been hell. We bicker and fight. We hurt each other's feelings. He says things. I say things. And the worst part is we mean them. It's not like we say things that we don't mean to get a reaction. I told him he was a selfish, self-absorbed douche bag the other day and he made my life miserable." Amone said.

"How did he respond to that?" Isabelle asked, eyebrows raised, as she pulled into the clinic parking lot.

"He left. He came back later, but didn't really talk to me. He picks at everything I do. Nothing is good enough anymore. Nothing makes him happy. Everything is just wrong," Amone said, relaxing into the seat, her neck turned toward Isabelle. "I'm physically exhausted by this process and I'm emotionally broken from trying so hard to be everything he wants and never measuring up. I may need to leave for him to miss me."

As much as Isabelle wished she knew what to say, she was at a loss for words, and was relieved they were at the clinic and would need to continue this conversation later.

"Well, we're here. Let's do this. We'll worry about the rest later, but right now, I'm here for you and you've been through too much to walk away without giving this everything you can."

"I suppose you're right. Let's do this," Amone said, unbuckling her seatbelt.

Isabelle's home landline phone rang. *No one ever calls on this phone.* Isabelle kept the phone for media interviews, mostly radio show interviews related to her novel, *The Kindness Project.*

"This is Isabelle Salton," she answered, without glancing down at the caller ID.

"I called you. I raised you. I know who you are," Harriet said.

Isabelle subconsciously fluttered her eyes, without an audience. It was a tick over which she had no control. "Good morning, Aunt Harriet, how are you today?"

Isabelle stood motionless, holding the phone, listening to details about fifteen different things Harriet shared before getting to the reason she called. There was a time when phone calls like this frustrated her to no end. But she was in a different place now – a place where she could better appreciate the small things and the idiosyncrasies of those she loved.

"I don't know. I haven't thought about Thanksgiving. It's two and a half months away. Why?" Isabelle answered.

Harriet proceeded to explain that the house she and Joy grew up in had recently been purchased by a family at her church, who had plans to turn it into a bed and breakfast. "How many rooms does it have?" Isabelle asked.

"Okay, I'm sure Zach and Amone are in. Do you want to call Carrie, or do you want me to? I'm guessing she would need to request time off well in advance from the hospital, but it's worth asking. She'd appreciate the invitation either way." Isabelle asked.

This Ellensburg thing is getting out of control. Isabelle had no desire to return to Ellensburg, mostly because she had no desire to see Owen again. But just as she didn't share with Harriet when she met him in Maui, she also didn't share her assessment of him leading her on while apparently cheating on the other woman in his life. *What a fabulous and dynamic guy he turned out to be.*

"Sure, Thanksgiving in Ellensburg sounds great," Isabelle said, despite her real feelings. She knew it was what Harriet wanted. And a part of her was curious to roam around the house her mom and Harriet grew up in as children, even if it looked completely different now.

Just as she hung up the phone, Grace walked into the kitchen, followed by Snoopy, which at some point had determined he was Grace's dog. "Hey," Isabelle said, trying to connect with her twelve-year-old. "Harriet just invited us to Thanksgiving at her place. What do you think of that?"

Grace walked over to a cupboard and took out Snoopy's

treat bag, "I guess it's okay if I get my own room." Grace laid down her parameters for attending the family celebration without making a fuss.

"According to Harriet, the house grandma and Yia Yia grew up in is being turned into a bed and breakfast, so I think we're probably going to stay there," Isabelle said.

"Awesome. Shared bathrooms," Grace said sarcastically.

"You look cute. Pink is your color." Isabelle complimented her daughter. She knew compliments always worked on her, so it was worth trying them out on Grace.

"Thanks, Mom. Our Young Life group is going to the movies this afternoon. Can I have twenty dollars?" Grace asked.

"I have cash in my purse. Grab what you need," Isabelle said. She took a deep breath. *It felt so good for Isabelle to be in a financial position to say this to her daughter.* She remembered a time not that long ago that purchasing grocery staples was a stretch. *The Kindness Project* had changed their lives, from the beginning when the original project helped them through a difficult Christmas, to now when the publication and sales of the book created a lifestyle that financially replaced all they had lost.

"Thanks mom," Grace said, kissing her mom on the cheek. Isabelle smiled. She had entered that uncomfortable space of parenting a pre-teen, and balancing her own need for her daughter's affection with her daughter's need for independence. Just as Grace was growing up and spreading her wings, Isabelle was developing the wisdom to know when to push forward and when to hold back.

Isabelle watched the mail truck pull away, and when she opened her front door she was startled to see Zach. "Oh, hi," she said. "Come in. I was just heading out to check the mailbox."

"So what was your assessment of the Ellensburg house

when you were there?" Zach asked.

"My assessment is that I'm done getting in the middle of this issue you have with Harriet spending her own money," Isabelle said. "Why do you care so much anyway?" Isabelle asked.

"Because she's not making a sound investment, and as her closest living relatives, don't you think we owe it to her to help her see what she's doing?"

"Nope." Isabelle replied. "But, I do have an opportunity for you."

"What's that?" Zach asked.

"She has invited all of us to Ellensburg for Thanksgiving, and you could use that time to sit down and tell her how you feel. Maybe you'd be more effective at helping her make a sound investment."

"You're being sarcastic, Izz, and frankly it's not that helpful right now," Zach said.

"Oh, poor Zach. I'm so sorry I'm not being helpful to you. Unlike your sarcasm, which is always so helpful for me," she said in a slightly snappy tone. "What do you want?" She asked seriously. "Why are you here bugging me about Harriet? You travel all the time. Why aren't you home with your wife?"

"That's a loaded question," he said.

Isabelle looked at him without any expression. *This is not good. They both want out.* Isabelle sighed. "Follow me. I'll make some coffee." Zach followed his sister into the kitchen and sat on the bar stool as Isabelle brewed two individual cups of coffee. "You still take yours black?" she asked as she poured a small amount of half and half in her own cup. Zach nodded affirmatively. "So?"

"I don't know where to start, Izz."

"You two were so happy. You fit together so perfectly.

When did things start to change?" Isabelle asked.

"She used to be gentle and loving and happy to see me. Now, it's like the sight of me nauseates her."

"Zach, she's on hormone therapy. Everything nauseates her."

"I know. But now she's bitter. I think it's this baby thing. I never needed kids. I mean, we have your kids and while Grace and Hope may be our nieces, we have them part-time and we still get to be adults and be spontaneous. But she wanted kids so I thought if it made her happy, fine." Zach exhaled and buried his face in his hands. *Is he going to cry?*

CHAPTER 8

Out of nowhere, Zach pounded the end of his fist on Isabelle's counter. "I'm sorry," he said. "I guess I am angry. I have given her the whole damn world and she accused me – me – of being selfish. What more can I give her? I just want to be her husband again and right now, even when we're civil, it's cold.

She doesn't touch me. She doesn't talk to me. She doesn't ask me how my day was? All she cares about are these stupid fertility treatments and when we have appointments. I go where she tells me to go, and do what I'm told to do, and she doesn't even really say thank you. We never have sex anymore. I masturbate in a stupid cup in a stupid clinic. If it works, then what? We separate and I pay child support for eighteen years? That's exactly what I wanted when I married the love of my life." Zach paused. He took a sip of coffee. "Glad you asked?"

Isabelle smiled. "Yep."

"I'm glad this amuses you. I'm glad my life falling apart makes you smile. You could pretend that you care that my life is imploding. When your life was imploding, I was there for you." Zach stood up.

"Zach, stop. I care deeply about you, Amone, and your marriage. You're right. You have seen me through the most devastating years of my life. There's nothing I wouldn't do for you or to help you. When you hurt, I hurt," Isabelle said.

"So why were you laughing at me," Zach said.

"I wasn't laughing at you. I am glad I asked and you finally opened up," she said, walking over to him, burying her head in his chest and clinging to his shirt. "You've helped me so much. I'm giddy thinking I might finally be in a position to help you."

Zach stepped back from his sister and sat back down. "You can help? Great. What's your big solution, Izz?" Zach asked.

"I'll talk to Amone. I think you guys are going to be okay," Isabelle said.

"We haven't been okay for a while," Zach said.

"Let me talk to her," Isabelle said, sincerely, placing her hand on the top of his to let him know she took his concerns seriously. Isabelle could see that her brother was overwhelmed with emotion.

"Izz, can we change the subject?" Zach asked. Isabelle smiled at him and nodded affirmatively.

"So, I had a book signing and Seattle. And while I was there, I saw Masingho," Isabelle said.

"That dude from college?" Zach asked. "Is he still a pot-head?"

"He smoked weed like three times. He wasn't a pothead. But anyway!"

"How'd it go?" Zach asked.

"Wonderful." Isabelle replied. "It was a gift that I wish had come in some form years ago," she said.

"Great. So are you moving to Portugal or is he moving to Portland?" Zach asked. Isabelle wrinkled her nose. She wasn't sure why he made this assumption, but she gave him some slack given everything he had going on.

"When he went home to Portugal, he promised to come back, but he never did. Would you believe I spent the last two decades fantasizing about him?" Isabelle paused for a few seconds, holding her brother's attention. "I actually dated Arnie to get over Masingho…"

Zach cut her off. "That guy? Really?"

"I got pregnant and Arnie and I got married."

"I was there." Zach rolled his eyes.

"Arnie was a fun boyfriend, and while he was mechanical and street smart, we struggled to communicate the way I always hoped. Every time Arnie and I fought or muddled through another disagreement, Masingho was always there, like a third person in our marriage, the safe, perfect fantasy in the back of my mind. Does this make sense?" Isabelle asked.

"Not even a little bit." Zach shook his head.

"Masingho wasn't perfect." Isabelle said, trying to get her point across.

"Perfect? He was an idiot," Zach said. "I gave you credit for seeing that."

"Zach, do you know why he came back? Why he reached out to me?"

"I'm sure to get back together. He probably heard you were single and now wealthy with your book. Old love. Add money. Dead husband. Sounds like the perfect set-up for an Act Two."

"No, not to get back together. He asked me to be his mistress – his in-town girlfriend when he was in Seattle." Isabelle said in a monotone voice, hoping to shock her brother.

Zach wasn't fazed. "Isn't that what I just said?" Zack responded. "Why do you make this so complicated, Izz?"

"He was my first love and he offered to put me up in an

apartment when he was in town."

"Which property?" Zach asked, moving his eyebrows up and down.

Grace appeared in the doorway. "Is everything okay?"

Isabelle wanted to sink into the floor. *What did Grace hear?* Without her mom asking the question aloud, Grace answered. "I heard everything. And honestly, I wish I hadn't. Can I go to the mall? Sabra's mom can pick me up and I'll be with her."

"Yes, tell Sabra you're welcome to hang out at the mall with her," Isabelle said.

"Great. Thanks," Grace said as she left the room.

"That was priceless. If the IVF is successful, I too could have a moment like that someday," Zach said. "Oh, but no, I wouldn't have that moment – because I wouldn't talk about my sex life with my kids around," Zach said. "But we're different."

"Are you finished, because I was actually making a super important point," Isabelle said.

"Of course. Your point. What was that?"

"Zach, I fantasized about a man who valued me so little that it took me twenty years to see he wasn't even capable of caring about me. And while it was twenty years wasted, I'm a different person today. I listen to my gut now. I trust myself enough to walk away when the old me would have probably, I don't know, maybe not been so smart."

"So I might as well just ask since I'm not a girl and I don't really know where you're going with this," Zach stated, leaving an awkward silence for Isabelle to fill.

"When you agreed to go through this in vitro process, did you lead Amone to believe you two were in this together?" Isabelle asked.

"Of course we're in this together. We're married and

ideally, we're making a baby, together," Zach said, stating the obvious.

"What if I can help you?" Isabelle said.

"How would you do that?" Zach asked.

"Your relationship has always worked because your roles were defined. You brought the masculine energy. She brought the feminine support. You loved her and she loved you back. But Zach, when it came to this IVF, you changed the game. You gave her permission to create a brand new little life with you and then you put it on her. She had to track the appointments and tell you when and where to show up, which you resented, as did she. Without even realizing it, you made her give up her femininity to take charge of this whole baby-making process. If you want to save your marriage, you need to be the man she married. You need to take charge of this IVF. Lead her, love her, and let her love you back. Be her husband and watch the woman you fell in love with reemerge," Isabelle said.

"Where did you read that? It's incredibly conservative from my super liberal sister," Zach said.

"I'm progressive. But this is not a political thing. Your relationship would be just as successful if you brought the feminine energy from the beginning and she brought the masculine energy. It's not about gender roles at al. It's about energy, defined relationship roles, and not changing the rules part-way into a relationship," Isabelle clarified.

"If you say so."

"You know I believe in women's rights, equal pay for equal work, gender equality and total control over our bodies. This has nothing to do with that. Zach, it doesn't matter which person in the relationship brings which energy. But the battery doesn't light up when it's not aligned. You are *lighting a birthday candle with a blow torch* masculine and you picked a woman who steps in *whatever direction you lead* feminine. And you loved that about her. When you put her in a position where she was forced to take charge of one of the most important decisions of your marriage, it challenged both your roles and in the process nearly broke your relationship. So fix it. You need to fix this, and you can."

Zach's spirit was searching. He was clinging to his sister's words. "How?"

"Figure it out. You're resourceful." Isabelle tipped her head to the side and pressed her lips together.

Zach stood up and started to walk toward the front door. But before he left the kitchen, he turned around, walked back to Isabelle and engulfed her in a gigantic bear hug. His tough and argumentative exterior cracked in two. As tears began to roll down his face, he tried to hide his emotions. He buried it into her long red hair. "You see why I couldn't let you die? I need you. How could I ever get through this without you?" he asked.

"Well, you did carry my mortgage until I could pay you back," she laughed.

"And I'd do it again," he said.

She cupped his face in her hands. "I know. I love you. Just remember there's a difference between masculine and macho. The second one is really annoying!" She smiled.

"I'll work on that," he said as he spun around.

"Hey! So Thanksgiving in Ellensburg? Can I tell Harriet you're in?"

"Sure. Sounds great," he said with glee.

"Zach?"

"What?" he said impatiently, wanting to get out the door.

"Lay off Harriet. It's her money. Let her spend it how she wants," Isabelle insisted.

"You got it." Zach waved as he rushed out the front door.

Isabelle watched the door that Zach had just walked through. Then she glanced over at the chair where Arnie used to sit. She smiled as she remembered how he used to spill his potato chips and how mad it made her at the time. *Oh Arnie, if only I knew then what I know now. I would have been such a better wife. Maybe we could have made it.*

"Babe. I always loved you just the way you are." The voice was coming from behind her. It was Arnie's voice but she knew he was dead. *Is Grace still here? Is Hope still napping?* She turned around. She smiled. It was so good to see him again, even if it was in her mind.

"I'm so sorry. I did the best I could at the time, but I'm so sorry, Arnie."

"I know. We all do the best we can, and when we know better, we do better," Arnie said.

Isabelle wanted to go over and hug him. She longed to feel his arms around her again. But she knew he wasn't physically there.

"Arnie, I need your help with something." Isabelle started to sob.

"Oh Babe, don't cry. You're doing such a great job. I'm so proud of you," Arnie said.

"I wish you hadn't left. The night you went for your clothes. I wish you hadn't left," Isabelle blubbered.

"I know," he said, his warm eyes welcoming her home to him.

"I wish you had paid the insurance money," she said.

"If I had, there never would have been *The Kindness Project*. I am sorry you had to suffer getting from there to here. We all walk through some type of fire in life. Mine was struggling to hang onto you the night in the ER when you were in the room, but the force pulling me away from you was just too strong. I wanted to stay. I tried to stay. But my time here was up."

Hearing these words, Isabelle held her breath, until she couldn't anymore and her body forced her to breathe again. She stared at Arnie, drinking in everything about him. She smiled. She put her palm to her mouth. *Oh, Arnie.* He was wearing one of her favorite shirts. It was the blue one she bought him – the one he wore the night he came for dinner to help Grace with her science project. It made her smile through the tears.

"I love you so much. I know I didn't always treat you lovingly. I was jealous and mad and probably a bit crazy, but I truly and completely loved you, Arnie."

He knew it. She could see he knew it by the smile on his face. "We have the most amazing daughters. You're such a great mom," he said.

"Arnie, I wish you could come back. I need you so much more than I ever realized. You were the light in my world and the fun in my day," she said. "Please come back."

"I need you to move forward. For you, for our girls, for me. I need you to forgive me and forgive yourself and just live every day as it comes," he said.

"Arnie, I lost your ring. I was surfing and I lost it in the water. I lost your wedding ring. I was so upset. I'm so sorry." Isabelle was still tortured by that day.

"You're gonna get my ring back." He promised.

"How? It's in the sea in Maui, or wherever the waves have taken it."

"Don't worry about it. Stop living in the future and the past. Just take each day as it comes. You'll be so much happier that way. I promise." His brown eyes served as the safe harbor she so desperately craved. Oh, she could get lost in his eyes. And she had – so many times when they were dating and first married.

"Izz, I can't tell you anything that will change your future," Arnie started, and then paused. "But trust me, you'll be okay. You'll be better than okay, love."

"Arnie, please," Isabelle prodded.

"You will find love again, and you're going to be happy. Trust that," Arnie predicted.

"I don't know. I feel so broken," Isabelle sighed while her eyes glassed over with tears.

"We're all broken in this life. Life doesn't break us. We come into life broken. It's only through acceptance, healing, and faith that we become whole again," Arnie shared.

"I like this philosophical side of you. I wish you didn't have to die to get here," she said jokingly.

"I was my very best self, of my entire life, the night of my car accident. You're still here because you have more to accomplish. Keep your head up and your heart open," he said.

"You wouldn't believe the two doozies who just crossed my path. Can you at least tell me who to look for or who to avoid?" Isabelle asked, hoping for a path she could finally trust.

"Sometimes the timing is off and what looks like the end of the story is simply a chapter break. Keep reading. The best endings are the ones you can't predict," he said. "I've already said way too much. Life is a series of choices and sometimes it takes a few tries for everyone to make the best choices at the same time."

Isabelle yawned as she inhaled a full breath of air, not because she was tired, but because it was so much to take in. "I need one thing more before you go," she said.

"What's that?" he asked.

"I know I can't hold you, but I just wish there was some way to connect physically again. If only I could feel you against me once more." Isabelle said, still emotional. "I'm so lonely, Arnie. I have the girls and Snoopy, but I'm still so lonely."

Arnie looked around the room. His eyes stopped on the oversized sofa. "I don't know if this will work, but let's try it," he said. She nodded, happy to agree to anything he asked. "Lie down on the sofa, on your side facing the back," he started. "Now cross your opposite hands to each shoulder to hug yourself. Close your eyes, Babe, close your eyes." Arnie laid down on the edge of the sofa to spoon her. "Can you feel me behind you?"

Isabelle silently nodded that she could. This time, she didn't cry. She felt completely engulfed in his love. Though she didn't realize it at the time, Isabelle had indeed experienced true and complete love. Lying here, she was reminded of it, where everything else in life, for this moment, faded to gray.

"Arnie, Harriet is looking for answers in mom and dad's house in Ellensburg. What can you tell me to help me better understand?" Isabelle asked.

"Your mom had the same gift that you and Grace have. She knew things. And she wrote them down in a diary. It's sealed in the walls of the house. Your dad put it there for safe keeping. You already know everything the book contains. You know they loved you and your brother so very much. At the end of life, that's all that matters, Izz. To truly love and be loved in return."

"I loved you, Arnie," Isabelle said. She felt so very tired. "I didn't tell you that enough."

"I love you too, Babe. Always did. Always will." Isabelle heard these words as she drifted off to sleep.

Suddenly, he was on top of her, licking her nose and shaking her. "Arnie, what are you doing?" she asked. When she opened her eyes, Hope was shaking her arm and Snoopy was standing on her torso, licking her face.

Ugh. I must have been dreaming. What a dream. She looked at Hope who had a scared look on her face. "Mommy, are you okay?"

"Yes baby girl. I guess I was just tired, so I took a nap." She wasn't ready to wake up. She wanted to go back to sleep. She wanted to feel Arnie against her again. But she heard his words replayed: *Stop living in the future and the past. Just take each day as it comes. You'll be so much happier that way. I promise.*

Isabelle sat up and pulled Hope close, cradling her little body. "Do you know how much I love you?" Isabelle squealed as she tickled her little girl. "This much," she quickly answered, stretching her arms out in each direction. "I love you infinitely."

Hope placed her fingers on Isabelle's upper lip. "Mommy, did you know you have a mustache?" Isabelle sighed. Isabelle reached up and felt the lightest patch of peach fuzz on her upper lip. *Ha! Note to self. Schedule a wax. Outta the mouths of babes.*

CHAPTER 9

Isabelle was spreading creamy peanut butter on gluten-free bread when her phone alerted her to an incoming text from Amone. The words "Just letting you know..." popped up on the preview screen. Isabelle finished the sandwich for Hope and cut the edge off the bread. "Come here love. I have your lunch ready," Isabelle called out.

After lifting Hope into her booster chair, Isabelle turned to reach for her phone. "May I have some milk?" Hope's question interrupted her reach.

"Sure honey." Isabelle walked over to her black stainless steel pro-style refrigerator with the insta-view door to get the milk for Hope. As she always did, she paused and smiled at the refrigerator just before reaching it. It was the first significant purchase she made after recovering from the financial despair that had rocked her world two and a half years earlier. The refrigerator was more than a year old but she was still so proud of it. It represented so much more than an appliance. Beyond looking what Isabelle considered to be cool, the insta-view door reminded her that their refrigerator was no longer empty. Every time she glanced at it, a full refrigerator reminded Isabelle that she could finally take care of the physical needs of her girls.

The phone sent a second alert. *I'm coming.*

After setting down the sippy cup in front of Hope, Isabelle returned to the counter to check her text messages: *Just letting you know I left the house. I left Zach a note. I'm staying at the Monaco. They let me bring Winnie. I just needed some space. Let me know if you want to catch the farmer's market on Monday. It's open through October.*

Isabelle's jaw dropped open. *October? This is only the end of September. Zach! What did you do?*

Isabelle texted back: *Is there anything I can do?*

Amone: *No. We just have to go through this.*

Isabelle: *Zach was here an hour ago. He was heading home. To you. To apologize.*

Amone: *I'm tired of him taking me for granted.*

Isabelle read Amone's message repeatedly, the way she would read the words from a man who broke up with her. Isabelle knew her brother loved his wife, but she also knew he could be self-centered; she related to Amone's frustration more than she would have preferred.

Noticing Hope had mostly finished her half peanut butter and jelly sandwich, she cleaned up her plate and offered a suggestion, "I think we need to take a little field trip to visit Auntie Amone."

Isabelle wasn't one to sit and text for hours. Zach and Amone had been there for her and she loved them enough to return the favor.

When Isabelle and Hope arrived to the Monaco in Pioneer Square, Isabelle drove up to the valet entrance. She opened the trunk to take out an oversized stroller for Hope. At three, Hope didn't need a stroller, but Isabelle still preferred one. It was so much easier than chasing her every time something caught her attention. Hope still fit in the stroller, and the back pocket offered the perfect pouch for Isabelle's purse. After sliding the valet stub into her purse, she pulled out her phone to text Amone: *Meet me in the lobby.*

Isabelle felt impatient over Amone's lack of prompt response. *Hello lady. It's your fav SIL. In the lobby. With a 3-y-o!* Isabelle sat back in the comfy, ornate sofas and waited for Amone's response. Isabelle reached over and picked up a glossy luxury travel magazine on an end table. She smiled as she thumbed through the pictures included in a feature story about Portugal. She set the magazine down on her lap, and tipped her head back with her eyes closed. *Twenty years. Twenty years and a million fantasies about a man who never existed.* She inhaled deep and slow, and exhaled just as measured.

"What are you reading?" Amone asked, startling Isabelle.

"Oh," Isabelle jumped.

"You were far far away." Amone observed, as she reached down and picked up the magazine. "Oh yes, of course, Portugal."

Amone sat down on the velvet chase next to Isabelle. "I've been losing him for a while. I've felt him pulling away, working late, just checking out. I think what really hurts is that he's not fighting to keep me. I told him where I was staying. He hasn't even called. He hasn't showed up. Just crickets. You called. You showed up uninvited."

"Did he know you were leaving?"

"I left a note. I checked in here a few hours ago. I just needed space," Amone said.

"Don't give up on my brother. Give him a chance to fix this, please," Isabelle pled.

"He's had months of chances," Amone responded.

"I know, but I think things are different. I talked to him today. He loves you. He told me so. And he wants a chance to be the husband you married and need him to be." Isabelle bit her lower lip.

"He told you that?" Amone asked.

. "Kinda. To be fair, Zach is not a girl. So he used different words but that's the message that came across," Isabelle winked.

Amone had a sad look in her eyes that Isabelle hadn't seen before. "Even leaving him didn't get his attention."

"You not only have his attention, you are the center of his universe. Please trust me on this. Look, I don't want to seem like I'm taking sides. I love you both. I want to help but I don't want to get in the middle and say something to inadvertently make things worse," Isabelle said. *How much should I tell her? Is it my place to tell her?* Isabelle struggled with how to respond. She could envision her brother getting quite angry if she crossed a line and over-shared with his wife, even if she and Amone were like sisters. "I know he loves you, more than anything. I know that," Isabelle said.

"Then why isn't he here? I'd cross an ocean for him but he can't even cross town for me. Why isn't he asking me to come home – telling me we can work it out?" Amone asked. Isabelle found it quite strange that the woman who normally understood men better than anyone was asking her questions about a man, even if it was her brother.

"Well, do you really want to know?" Isabelle asked.

"Yes," Amone responded enthusiastically.

"Because men are weird." Isabelle smiled. She was trying to be funny but clearly her joke fell flat.

"I hate that you're doing this. Zach does this. He makes a joke out of things that aren't funny," Amone said, crossing her arms in front of her chest.

"I'm sorry. Look, Zach was at my house. He left minutes before your text came in. He can be tough and hard-headed. But he's my brother and I know without a doubt he loves you more than anyone and yes, he would cross an ocean for you too. I know that about him." Isabelle was serious.

"So why hasn't he called?" Amone asked.

Isabelle knew the answer, but she didn't want to seem like a know-it-all so she responded simply. "Give him a chance." She watched Amone look off into the distance, and she wanted desperately to help.

"Every time he ignores me, he's teaching me to live without him. I can't believe I wanted to make a baby with him. I thought what we had was real." Amone was despondent. Isabelle had never seen her this way.

"How about this? You probably don't feel like eating, but let's just stroll around downtown and maybe grab a coffee or stop in at Powell's." Thumbing through isles of books at Powell's Bookstore always made Isabelle relax and she hoped it might help Amone. "But you should grab a jacket. It's a little cool out there for what you're wearing. Hope and I will wait while you run upstairs."

Amone nodded. "Okay," she said, standing up. "I'll be right back."

While Amone was gone, Isabelle text messaged Zach. *I'm with Amone. She's sad but she's okay. I think you should show up tomorrow morning. Or tonight. Surprise her. Show her you care.*

Zach shot back: *Stop meddling.*

Isabelle: *You asked for my help. Reassuring your wife that you love her is not meddling. You should thank me.*

Zach: *I'll text her later. Pls butt out.*

Isabelle: *Real men show up. Texting is for chickens. Peck, peck, peck.*

Zach: *Isn't there some asshole an ocean away you would be better off obsessing about?*

Isabelle: *You're a jerk.*

Zach did not respond, which was just as well as Amone walked up to Isabelle and Hope, jacket folded over one arm, and a leash to their always meticulously groomed Doberman pincer, Winnie, in the other. Isabelle kneeled down to greet Winnie as she simultaneously slipped her phone back into the side pocket of her purse with her free hand. *No wonder she left him.* Isabelle looked directly at Amone and smiled, as if nothing was going on. "I could really use an Americano," Isabelle said.

Pushing Hope's stroller with the toddler nestled inside, Isabelle walked quietly beside Amone out the front doors and down Washington. Even with the added weight from IV-therapy, Amone was a beautiful woman, and next to the stately dog, she turned heads on every block. While there was a time she might have felt jealous or competitive, finally confident in her own skin, Isabelle didn't mind being somewhat invisible next to her sister-in-law. Isabelle watched in admiration as several onlookers glanced at Amone and smiled.

"My brother will come around, but if he doesn't, I think you might still have your pick of Portland men," Isabelle said, as she nudged Amone gently with her elbow. Amone looked down at her but didn't say anything. "The thing is this, love is more like an ocean than a mountain. The tides move in and out. There are storms, some that wash up some ugly debris. There are gentle, warm waves that invite play. People in love drift together and apart continually," Isabelle paused. She wanted to give her words a chance to sink in. "I wish I had realized that while Arnie was alive. I'm not sure if he was my soul mate or simply one of the great loves of my life. But I have come to realize that while there were times when we clearly drifted apart emotionally and physically, there was always an underlying connection. The true love we shared with each other was always there on some level, waiting to reignite."

"That's interesting," Amone said. Isabelle wasn't sure if

she really thought that or was just saying it to be polite.

"Which part resonates with you?" Isabelle asked her pointedly.

"Things seemed pretty impossible with you and Arnie the last few weeks before his accident but obviously you worked things out enough to have Hope." Isabelle didn't quite understand what Amone was getting at.

"Do you know what the biggest barrier was to a great relationship with Arnie and me? Well there were a few things, but do you know the biggest one?" Isabelle asked.

"You nagged him a lot and he disappointed you." Amone guessed.

Wow! That sounds bad! "Those were symptoms. There were three people in our marriage the entire time. Arnie, me and a stupid fantasy I had about a guy I dated in college – who I thought was incomparably amazing and impressive," Isabelle said.

"Zach told me about the foreign exchange student who broke your heart," Amone said.

"Yes, Masingho seemed amazing but he wasn't. Arnie didn't seem that amazing but he was. He was an awesome dad. He was fun. He loved me even though I drove him crazy. He ignored me sometimes, which drove me nuts but probably that's what allowed him to love me so much. He wasn't terribly responsible. He didn't take charge like I thought I wanted. He rolled with life. And if I hadn't been comparing him to this ideal fantasy man in my mind, I might have found he was actually the best friend and lover I truly needed and wanted. Would you believe there was never a time I initiated sex and he turned me down?"

"So now that you know the truth about Masingho, are you replacing him with Arnie, up on that pedestal to which no one else can compare?" Amone asked.

"I'm not sure I understand what you're suggesting," Isabelle insisted.

"Are you using your appreciation for your deceased husband to keep a wall around your heart so no new man can possibly measure up to Arnie the same way Arnie was never able to measure up to Masingho?" Amone asked.

Isabelle laughed. "You know men do not have these kinds of conversations, right?"

"I know. But it's worth considering." Amone said. "Have you talked to Owen?"

"Oh that guy. No. What's there to say?" Isabelle asked.

"You had a connection with him. You can't deny that," Amone proposed. Isabelle simply shook her head slowly side-to-side.

"Maybe my life is full without a man. Maybe I'm at a point where I have my girls. I have my family. I have my writing. I love me and that's enough," Isabelle said.

"Well, if that's truly the case, I support you. But I think, and this is just a hunch, that one day, you'll open the door or bump into your forever Mr. Right when you least expect it. Your guard will be down and everything you wanted, but weren't yet ready for, will be standing in front of you. And I think when that happens, you'll say yes. And you won't need to fantasize about Masingho or Arnie anymore because your heart will have found the love it longs for," Amone sighed. "That's what I hope for you."

Isabelle wanted Amone to be right. "I guess we can check back twenty-five years from now and see how close you came. Honestly, there was a time I would have wanted and even sought that, but I guess I've found a genuine peace with myself where I'm enough. Even without a man, I'm enough." Isabelle surprised herself with her passionate declaration for solitude. "You know it's strange, Amone, Arnie has visited me more than once since his accident. We've shared some of the best conversations of our entire relationship and I think we're better friends today than when he was alive. I think if I could have anyone in my life I would choose to have him back," Isabelle said.

"I dated a man in my twenties who was gay. He was the best friend and boyfriend, and honestly, I was shocked when he came out. We went our own ways and then one day I ran into him and we picked up right where we left off. He made me laugh so hard I nearly peed my pants. We exchanged contact information and he became one of my best friends for many years," Amone shared. "You once asked my secret about how I understand men so well. Bryan is my secret. He's the man who taught me how to understand and relate to men."

"I guess he'd know," Isabelle said. "Why haven't I met this fabulous Bryan?"

"He died in a motorcycle accident about a year before I met Zach. I still talk to him all the time. So I get it. Gay guys, dead guys, even married guys – they are all safe. And they make the best friends. But what if there's someone out there who's available in every way and he loves you, and you love him, and what if, you get to stop talking to your memories and yourself? Why wouldn't you want that?" Amone asked.

Isabelle had to look away. She didn't want Amone to see her tear up. "Food for thought. There's Spella's. Have you been there? They make the best coffee. Let's head that way," Isabelle said, changing the subject. Amone knew what she was doing and simply followed along. Her point had been made.

CHAPTER 10

A month later, it was time for another Ellensburg adventure. As Isabelle pulled into Harriet's driveway, she looked into her rear view mirror with complete contentment as she watched both her girls sleeping in the backseat. She could have stayed and just watched them sleep if only her full bladder wasn't screaming at her for relief. Even still, for just a moment, before she unfastened her seatbelt, she sat in amazement and gazed at her girls, as her heart filled with gratitude. *They may not be perfect, but they are mine, and I really couldn't ask for more.* She inhaled an entire lungful of air and exhaled slowly.

She turned her head gently to the left and gazed out her driver's side car window at the maple trees decorated majestically with deep hues of red, orange and yellow that lined the street where Harriet lived – the same familiar street she called home as a little girl. *I can't believe there are still leaves out here with all this wind.* Suddenly, nature called and she really had to go to the bathroom. Now.

Instead of waking the girls, she turned off the car, left her door open and hustled toward Harriet's front door, which by the time she arrived, was open with Harriet waiting to greet her family. "Excuse me," Isabelle said as she wiggled by Harriet into the house.

"Well hello," Harriet said, perplexed at Isabelle's unusual

informality. Seconds after Harriet made her way to the car, and opened the door for Grace to hop out, Isabelle was back outside at the car to join them. "Sorry. That water ran right through me. I normally stop at the bathrooms on Snoqualmie Pass, but with the girls sleeping, I didn't want to wake them," Isabelle said.

Hope was now awake and Grace already had her overnight bag out of the car. "How was your drive?" Harriet asked.

"It was good. You know I love this time of year. The pass is magnificent with the evergreens and turning foliage."

"Too bad you're turning around to go back to Portland tomorrow," Harriet said.

"It's fine. I had stuff for Thanksgiving so the car isn't so packed when we come. And of course we wanted to see you, Aunt Harriet!" Isabelle added.

"Of course you did, dear. I have a roast simmering, with potatoes and carrots and onions. I was going to make a salad but I didn't get that far," Harriet said. "I baked an apple pie for later. Gluten-free for you."

"I love your apple pies," Isabelle said. "Thank you." Isabelle didn't eat a lot of sweets but she did appreciate the effort Harriet made and she wanted to be sure she knew that.

Isabelle was filling drinking glasses with ice and water in the kitchen with Grace and Hope when the doorbell rang. Isabelle looked around and didn't see Harriet. "I bet Harriet got locked out," Isabelle uttered aloud, as she made her way to the front door. She couldn't have been more surprised when she opened the door. It wasn't Harriet.

"Hey, how are you?" the deep male voice asked.

That guy. "Hi," Isabelle said, with a forced smile, trying to be polite.

"I saw your car in the driveway, so I thought I'd see if you were here," Owen said.

"I drove it here," Isabelle said, half sarcastically, and half as a matter of fact.

Owen tipped his head, not sure what to make of her abrupt responses. Just then, Harriet showed up in the doorway behind Isabelle. "Oh it's your friend. I made a pot roast in my Instant Pot, and potatoes and carrots and onions. Do you use an Instant Pot?" Harriet asked Owen.

"A what?" Owen asked.

"It's an electronic pressure cooker that takes the guessing out. Would you like to join us for dinner?" Harriet invited Owen to stay. Isabelle could hardly interrupt to say no. She cringed inside.

"Oh that's very kind, but I just saw Isabelle's car and thought I'd stop by to say hello," Owen said.

"Well I still need to make gravy and a salad, but dinner should be ready in 20 minutes if you change your mind." Harriet invited Owen a second time.

"He really can't stay." Isabelle tried to give Owen an out. Grace walked into the living room, sat on the sofa and picked up a magazine. *Do I introduce them? I better.*

"Owen, this is my oldest daughter, Grace. Grace, Owen." Isabelle offered.

"Hi," Grace said without looking up.

"Nice to meet you, Grace," Owen responded.

"Grace, can you be a little more hospitable?" Isabelle asked. She hadn't intended for Grace to meet the professor, but since it happened, she at least wanted her daughter to appear to have manners.

Grace walked over to Owen and formally put out her right hand to shake his. "Nice to meet you, Sir," Grace said with a mixture of politeness and sarcasm. Isabelle overlooked this.

"Could we maybe walk and talk a few minutes?" Owen asked Isabelle. "I'll have you back in time for dinner," he promised.

Isabelle didn't really know how to say no, so she reluctantly grabbed her jacket from the back of the chair near the door and assured Harriet she would be back before dinner.

Owen held the screen door and opened the gate to the front sidewalk. Even though Isabelle was no longer smitten with him, she appreciated his polite gestures. The fall air was mostly warm with an underlying crispness. "I wasn't really expecting to see you again," Isabelle said. Despite having initially found him attractive, in Maui and Ellensburg, the fact that he was living with another woman made him off limits and unattractive in her mind.

"Look, I owe you an explanation – and I have something for you. I mean I don't have it with me, but I have something for you. I wanted to give it to you at the restaurant, before we got interrupted and you rushed out," he said, as they walked side-by-side with their arms frequently brushing.

Probably some book on fish hatcheries. No thanks. "Look, you don't owe me any explanations," Isabelle said. "And you don't need to give me anything. I've known men like you and I'm not interested."

"Men like me?" Owen asked. "Do you know who I am?"

"Yes, I know who you are. I was listening. I'm not interested in some local big shot who juggles women and plays the field. I'm not your type," she said.

"Big shot? I'm a college professor."

"In a college town. I get it. Why are you here, Owen? Why did you stop?" Isabelle was ready to turn around and walk the block back to Harriet's house alone. In fact, just to prove a point, she physically circled one hundred and eighty degrees to face in the other direction and took one step.

"Wait," he said, softly. She stopped.

"I'm listening," she said, keeping her back to him.

"Look, I don't have a girlfriend. I'm just a guy who's trying to save the world. Okay, not the world, but the water ladders here in Central Washington. They impact everything from the fish to Native American tribes and farmers' water rights and irrigation. They literally affect everyone," Owen said.

Isabelle looked at him with a dumbfounded expression. "You're just a guy who's trying to save the world?"

"Yes. Yes." Owen said.

Isabelle started to laugh. "Do you think I'm an idiot or are you completely delusional? And, and, and, what exactly does this have to do with your girlfriend-not-girlfriend-whatever-she-is, you somehow forgot to mention sooner?"

"I'm a mechanical engineer," Owen started.

"Fast forward." Isabelle said, unimpressed.

"Jill is a patent attorney and we are working together on a project. I developed a device that maintains the water temperature in fish ladders when the water is moved to and from reservoirs but I needed to patent it to prevent it from getting..."

"... stolen. I get it. I don't care," Isabelle said.

"But you should," Owen said. "Wait. I'm saying everything wrong. My friend is a patent attorney and she lived in Seattle. She was in bad relationship. I basically helped her out and told her she could stay with me. At the most, we were friends who blurred a few lines."

"So you had an understanding?" Isabelle asked.

"She was helping me with a critical project that will impact our whole state in a spectacular way. And with water being the scarce commodity that it actually is, it could help the world. I guess to answer your question, we've gotten together but we're not together," Owen explained.

"Is that how she sees it?" Isabelle asked.

"It's hard to say. Women see things differently than men. You know what I mean." Isabelle knew exactly what he meant. *So she thinks they're together, business and intimate partners, and he's banging her for free legal advice. What a great guy.*

"How truly romantic... said no woman ever, to a story like that." Isabelle was disgusted and it was written all over her face. "I don't really know you and I don't care who you date or get together with to save the world. Look, Owen, you're handsome, and clearly a local hero, at least when it comes to volunteer firefighting. I wish you well but I don't see that there's really anything here with us," she said, taking a step back.

In that moment, Owen had no choice. Nothing he said would make a difference. So he reached out and took her shoulders in his hands and pulled her close to him. He kissed her. He kissed her like she had never been kissed before. She wanted to resist, to push him away, but she couldn't. As unexpected as it was, she enjoyed his kiss far too much to reestablish her own space. Her body softened and her chest pressed into his as she gave herself permission to fully kiss him back, and enjoy it.

They were interrupted by a compact car, a block north of them, screeching away. "That was unexpected," Isabelle said, looking up.

"It's part of living in a college town," Owen said, stretching his neck long in an effort to see the car that had already rounded the corner.

"The kiss was unexpected. Not the car," Isabelle said, clarifying. She couldn't stop herself from smiling.

"Hopefully it won't be our last," Owen said.

"Harriet is probably ready for dinner," Isabelle said.

Owen and Isabelle walked back the few blocks to Harriet's house. "To be continued?" he asked flirtatiously, winking.

"If you're lucky," she said playfully in return. She tried to hide it but clearly enjoyed flirting with him. *I don't know about this guy.* She tried to hide her internal sigh. *I wish I didn't enjoy kissing him so much.*

"I'll take it," Owen said, reaching down to take her hand and draw it to his lips and kiss her hand goodbye. "You can trust me," he said, nodding. He could sense her trepidation, but was determined to win her over.

I want to trust you but I don't know. Still smiling, Isabelle gently pulled back her hand. "Time will tell, Professor. Time will tell," she said as she turned and walked toward the house. Isabelle could tell there was still something Owen wanted to say, but she didn't want to ruin the moment by over-thinking it or over-engaging in dialogue. She wanted to walk away still tasting his lips. She waved goodbye, turned and walked into the house.

"I wondered if you got lost," Harriet said, as Isabelle shut the front door.

"I'm sorry. Time got away from me," Isabelle said, still distracted by the kiss.

"It's been twenty-two minutes. You were going to be back in twenty," Harriet looked at Isabelle. "Are you flush? I do believe you are. Your face is red. You're flush!" Harriet noticed.

"I suppose it's the chill in the air," Isabelle said, not wanting to address her attraction to Owen.

"Go ahead and wash. I'm just dishing up," Harriet said.

* * *

The next morning, Harriet was already up with KCTS, the public broadcasting station, blaring in the kitchen, when Isabelle wandered out. "Good morning, sunshine," Harriet said loudly, above the television volume, just as Isabelle's phone alerted of an incoming text.

"Good morning, Harriet," Isabelle said, looking down at the message on her phone from Owen. *Meet me at Utopia for coffee at 8?* Isabelle was simultaneously pleased and disenchanted. She enjoyed the attention but would have preferred he waited more than 12 hours to try to see her again.

"Are the girls still sleeping?" Harriet asked, emphasizing the word still.

"It's 6:20 in the morning. Yes they're still asleep." Isabelle said. *Although I don't know how they are with the television this loud.* Over the years, Isabelle had learned to filter what came out of her mouth when it came to Harriet. The two women had made their peace over the years, largely due to Isabelle's ability to manage up. She had learned this skill with Sal at the insurance company. "I have an appointment at eight. Do you mind watching the girls? It shouldn't take that long."

"Sure. Where is your appointment on a Saturday?" Harriet asked, just as Isabelle knew she would, and had already come up with an answer before she asked her aunt for help.

"The tire shop. I need to have the stem checked on one of my tires. I think it's fine but I just want to be sure. It's when they could fit me in." Isabelle didn't like lying to Harriet, or anyone really, but it was easier than fielding a barrage of questions. She had come to see these white lies as an investment in her relationship with Harriet, as they prevented Harriet from asking too many intrusive questions and Isabelle from getting mad over Harriet's nosiness.

"No problem. How long will you be?" Harriet asked.

"Not sure." Isabelle said. Ambiguity was always her friend when it came to her aunt. Harriet seemed fine with this. *Awe, see, everybody wins.* "I'm going to take a shower," Isabelle announced as she turned to leave the room.

"Shall I make coffee?" Harriet asked.

"I'll get some on the way." *Now all I have to do is stop at the tire shop and everything I've said is true. Nice.* Isabelle seemed pleased with herself for finding a way to pull the entire situation together. *Is Owen really that hung up on me that he has to see me every day? Stop it. You like it. Even if you're not crazy about him.*

Isabelle arrived to Utopia a few minutes early. She enjoyed the quaint atmosphere of the boutique coffee shop. It reminded her of something in the theatre district in Portland. She looked at the sign, taking her time ordering to give Owen a chance to show up. *For being so excited to see me he's sure taking his time getting here.* A slightly eccentric-looking, short redhead with glasses formed a line behind Isabelle, waiting for her to order. Having recently added red highlights herself, Isabelle noticed other redheads the way she noticed people who drove her same model of car.

So as not to be obvious about checking out her hair, she turned and invited the woman to jump the line. "Go ahead. I'm waiting for someone," Isabelle said, nonchalantly.

"Thanks," the orange brassy redhead said, playing with a chain around her neck.

Isabelle stalled a few more minutes by walking over to hang her denim jacket on the back of a wooden chair at a small table. Suddenly, her mind played back a visual she saw but didn't reconcile in the moment. *The ring. The chain had a ring. Arnie's ring? No. I mean, it couldn't have been! I lost that ring in the ocean while I was surfing.*

Feeling awkward and embarrassed, Isabelle walked back over to the redhead. Looking down at her ring finger, Isabelle noticed a lovely emerald cut engagement ring. "This is going to sound nuts and I'm sorry to even be asking this. I noticed you have a ring on your chain and I lost one while surfing. I know this is so crazy but it looks like my late husband's ring," Isabelle said, and paused, waiting for the woman to fill in the details.

"Oh, I understand," she said, picking up her coffee from the counter, turning and walking toward a table on the other side of the room behind the counter.

"Is this ring special to you?" Isabelle asked.

"Yes, my fiancé gave it to me," she said proudly, reminding Isabelle of a slightly deranged Cupie doll.

"Would you mind checking the inscription? I'm so sorry to ask this. My late husband's ring was inscribed with the words *My Dear Love* on the inside of the band. I lost the ring surfing. It's possible someone found it and sold it to a jewelry store. It's possible your fiancé bought it without ever knowing it belonged to someone else." Isabelle worked hard to not let her emotions show.

"Oh how awful," the woman said, reaching up to take off the chain. "Owen gave me this ring to wear around my neck until our wedding day when I'll place it on his finger," she said taking off the chain.

"Owen?" Isabelle asked.

"He's a wonderful man; he'd be so upset to find out we were sold someone else's ring." The redhead sounded sincere, despite her exaggerated mannerisms. Isabelle wasn't sure what to believe. When she handed Isabelle Arnie's ring, Isabelle felt a surge run through her body.

"This ring belonged to my late husband. I'll pay you for it," Isabelle offered.

"Are you sure it was his?"

"Yes. It's the exact inscription. Wait. Did you say your fiancé's name is Owen?" Isabelle asked.

"Yes. Owen Mallinger. He's a professor at CWU," the orangish redhead said proudly, with a toothy, wide-grinned smile. "If this is really your ring, I guess it would only be right if I gave you the chance to buy it back. I don't know what Owen paid for it."

Suddenly, Isabelle felt terrible for the woman, who Isabelle now judged as less deranged and almost cute, in a grown-up Cabbage Patch Kid sort of way. *That jerk is playing us both. This has to be Jill. Owen has had Arnie's ring since I lost it. And he gave it to her? He didn't return it to me? What kind of a sicko is he?* Isabelle kept her cool and reached for her checkbook. "How about $300?" Isabelle asked.

"If that's all it's worth to you, that's fine. I'm sure he paid at least that," said the woman.

Without saying a word, Isabelle wrote out a check for five hundred. What's your name? For the check."

"You can just make it to cash," the woman suggested. "I'm sorry for your loss." While the woman shared her unusual brand of empathy, Isabelle returned the chain and ring to its rightful place – on her own neck. Something doesn't feel right. Isabelle got a hunch that something fishy was up, only she couldn't pinpoint who was playing her, exactly.

"Oh no. I want to make it to your fiancé, since he bought this ring, you said. Owen Mallinger. I mean he put all this cash out. I just want to see it go back to him," Isabelle said, enjoying watching the woman in front of her start to squirm.

Isabelle felt certain Owen was guilty; now she was trying to determine if this woman was in on this cruel extortion plan. "You know, I just realized I know Owen Mallinger. In fact, I'm meeting him here for coffee. He should be here any minute. How about if we all have coffee together, and I give him this check myself?"

The doll-looking redhead adjusted her glasses on her nose. Isabelle placed her hand over the ring, guarding the woman from reaching up and grabbing it back. The redhead sighed before she started to speak, suddenly with a slight stutter. "Uh, uh, on second thought, I'm sitting here thinking, uh, feeling the pain you must be experiencing and knowing this is one of those moments when I have a chance to do something incredibly selfless. You lost your husband and his ring. It's the least I can do to just give it back to you. I don't want to take your money. Just pay it forward," she said tipping her head to the side and forcing a slight smile.

"I intend to do that, to pay it forward," Isabelle said.

In fact," Jill continued, "he's not that observant. I'll buy a new ring and let's just keep this between us. I don't want him to feel bad about skimping on a secondhand ring. He's so proud." Jill picked up her purse and started backing up toward the door. "You be well," she said, backing out the door and rushing to her car.

Isabelle was floored. *Lady, you do not seem very smart for being an attorney.* Owen still hadn't showed up. *Did he have my ring and give it to another woman? Where are you? Why aren't you here?* Isabelle decided to text him. *Where are you?*

He wrote back a few minutes later. *Sorry I got delayed. Let's connect later.*

She read his text over a few times. *Owen! Did you find Arnie's ring in Maui?*

He wrote back: *How did you find out?*

Isabelle: *That's your response? How did I find out?* Isabelle was suddenly angry. She dialed his number. It went to voicemail.

He wrote back: *I can't talk. But I'm sorry. I understand if you never want to speak to me again. What I did was horrible.*

Isabelle stood in the coffee shop in complete disbelief. She sent one final text: *Never contact me again.* And once she saw the message was delivered, she blocked his number. *Owen Mallinger, you are dead to me!*

CHAPTER 11

*WEEKEND BEFORE THANKSGIVING
– ELLENSBURG, WASH.*

Grace enjoyed riding shotgun and choosing her favorite music to play via the Bluetooth on the trip to Ellensburg for Thanksgiving. She knew all the lyrics and happily sang along while Isabelle drove.

"Is Yia Yia going to be sad we're not staying with her?" Grace asked.

"No honey, she set this whole thing up. She's excited to have everyone in town, and although she probably wouldn't admit it, I bet she's stoked about not having to cook Thanksgiving dinner herself this year," Isabelle said.

"Who's going to cook?" Grace asked.

"I imagine it will be the family who owns the B&B, although, I'm sure we'll all pitch in and help. They're friends of Yia Yia's from her church." Isabelle's explanation seemed to sufficiently answer Grace's questions and she returned to singing with her music.

Isabelle and the girls usually stayed with Harriet while in Ellensburg, but this week was special. Isabelle was excited to have the gang all staying together at Ellensburg's newest bed and breakfast at her grandparents' former farm. Harriet reserved all the available rooms as soon as she heard about the opening from the new owners who attended Calvary Baptist with her.

"Turn left in twenty-five feet," the GPS on Isabelle's phone commanded. When the car arrived to the long driveway, Isabelle was suddenly flooded with memories of riding her bike along this same path. It was paved today, whereas she remembered falling and skinning her knee pretty badly one time on the gravel road that preceded it. She could still see her Grandma Mae on the front porch with her white ruffled apron and Grandpa James riding around the property on his tractor. She drove slowly, taking it all in. It had been years, so many years, since their grandparents passed away and Zach and Isabelle visited the farm.

Despite the changes that had been made over time, Isabelle felt a sense of familiarity. *It's like I was just here yesterday.*

When she pulled into the guest stalls at the front of the old house, she noticed Harriet's car. *Of course she's here to greet us. Very sweet.* Isabelle smiled. *We've come so far, Harriet, it's hard to believe. It's like we've lived a whole lifetime. Whatever would I have done if the stroke had taken you four years ago? But here we are. We made it together.* Just then, Harriet stepped out on the porch and waved. Isabelle excitedly waved back as she opened her driver-side door.

Grace climbed out of the car from the backseat and stretched before reaching for her suitcase. Her demeanor had changed so much the last year. Isabelle couldn't be sure how much of this was related to what happened at school and how much was simply the natural progression of adolescence.

Isabelle released Hope from her car seat and picked up the three-year-old.

"I have a surprise for you," Harriet said as Isabelle

climbed the steps.

"A good surprise?" Isabelle asked. She was joking but there was some truth behind her sense of hesitancy. Harriet had been known to meddle and the last person Isabelle wanted to see was Owen. She smiled and held her breath, praying she could be polite, while Harriet led her inside the bed and breakfast.

Isabelle's jaw dropped when she saw who was waiting for her in the reception room. It caught her completely off guard, and all she could do was silently sway her head side-to-side. "Oh my gosh, what are you doing here? I mean, it's great to see you but what brings you to Ellensburg?" she asked in complete disbelief.

Agus stepped toward her as Sal stood up. "Our daughter and her husband just opened this B&B.   Isabelle," Agus paused, "We're here because of you."

"I don't understand. We could have met for lunch in Portland. It's great you're here but what a long drive for you." Isabelle was confused.

"No, we're here, for Thanksgiving, because of your kindness project," Agus was solemn with a sense of complete peace about herself. *Is she referring to my book?* "This is our first holiday together as a family since Tim died. When Grace invited me to join you for your kindness project, I realized it was time to bring our family together again to celebrate holidays, to build new traditions, and to live."

By this time, Sal was standing next to Isabelle with his hand resting gently on her upper arm. "We lost our son but in our grief, we failed to celebrate the family we still had. This year, we're joining Alexa and Olivia for our first holiday together as a family since the accident," Agus said.

"And when we get home, we're putting up a tree," Sal added.

The magnitude of the moment and what Agus was saying hit Isabelle all at once, and she started to tremble. Tears of joy began to trickle down her face. She fully understood how much this meant to Agus and she got to be a part of it. The hell she lived through the past four years had not only made her a better person, it had made a significant and permanent difference in the lives of those she loved. Her response to great loss and pain, through *The Kindness Project*, helped ease the grief of her dearest friends, and all the while she had no idea. A flat but sincere smile widened horizontally across her face as she filled her lungs with air, slowly, the way she had so many times in her Pilates classes. A deep satisfaction penetrated her soul: *My great sadness was all for good.* She could not have explained this relief in mere words, but she felt it throughout every cell of her being.

The success of her book was certainly affirming. She admittedly relished the sales, attention, lifestyle and of course the recognition of being on the New York Times Bestsellers List. But nothing could compare to actually changing the life of someone she loved.

Isabelle hugged them both. "How perfect to have you here with us for Thanksgiving," Isabelle said.

"Well dear, it hasn't been an easy road getting here, but we made it through with the support of each other. I never dreamed I'd see this day," Agus said

"Say, Sal, I need to ask you something. I've just been dying to know. What was in the box?" Isabelle asked.

"The box?" Sal questioned, as if to throw Isabelle off course. She didn't say a word. She looked him straight in the eyes and ever so slightly she shook her head side to side. Sal sighed. "The keys to this B&B. The keys to our family coming together again," Sal said.

"I didn't sneak into an office building in the dark of night to get a box with the key to a B&B," Isabelle said.

"No, but you made it possible," Sal replied.

"What was in the box?" Isabelle demanded. Sal looked at Agus, who nodded her approval to tell Isabelle the truth.

"The company was cooking the books. They weren't buying insurance for everyone who paid in, gambling that the healthiest clients wouldn't access their insurance. When they had a claim for a preventative service, the company paid it as if the premium was in full effect. And I kept proof. I retired just before a DOJ investigation. I handed it over as part of a reward for information leading to the imprisonment of the fat cats who went to prison," Sal said.

"Holy cow! That's like mafia crap, Sal," Isabelle said.

"Yes. I was a whistleblower, and I'd do it again. It gave me the leverage to go to bat for my employees with confidence and ensure my family was cared for. You can see if I hadn't come through, and the information had fallen into the wrong hands, it could have been really bad," Sal said. Isabelle stood there looking at him, eyes wide and mouth open but silent. "It was only fair that if the information could have put my family in danger, the reward needed to be used to bring us all back together. Agus and I agreed to use the money as a down-payment to invest in a place that would give our family a second chance," Sal seemed pretty proud of himself.

"And you sent me in there, at night, to get it?" Isabelle was horrified, and she wasn't joking around. "I have small children, Sal, and you sent me for information that people may have killed for if they knew it existed."

"I'm sorry, Isabelle. You were the only person I trusted," Sal said.

Isabelle was not amused. She looked down, shook her head and turned to go find her guest room for the next week. Despite knowing the truth, *that helping Agus and Sal that night possibly saved her life by taking her mind off of the desperate situ-*

ation in which she found herself, Isabelle was not flattered by Sal's confidence.

"Isabelle?" Sal called after her. Agus lifted her arm out to stop Sal from following her.

"Give her time," Agus said. "She will come around."

Two nights later, drinks were served at The Porch with most of the group present: Isabelle, Zach, Amone, Carrie, Richard, Liberty, and Olivia. Isabelle's phone rang. Only she didn't hear it the first, second or third time it rang, above the lively roar of the bar. Isabelle enjoyed having her makeshift family together for the holidays. In some ways, although she was now middle-aged, this gathering of friends and family made her feel young again.

When Isabelle looked up, she noticed Agus enter the restaurant section of the establishment, below the bar, and she waved her over. Not one to hold grudges for long, Isabelle was over her misunderstanding with Sal.

Agus rushed to the table. "Isabelle, you need to come with me. Sal and I are on our way to Harriet's. There's been a fire. I tried to call you several times but I only got your voicemail."

"A fire? What? Is everyone okay?" Isabelle asked.

"Just come now," Agus said picking up Isabelle's purse and handing it to her.

"What's going on?" Zach asked.

Already in motion away from the table, Isabelle called back, "A fire at Harriet's. I'll see you there."

When Agus and Isabelle reached the front door, Sal had the car idling at the curb. Isabelle jumped into the backseat and Agus moved as quickly as she could at her age to scoot herself into the front passenger seat.

"Are the girls safe? Is Harriet okay? Did everyone get out?" Isabelle asked.

"I don't know. Madison didn't say," Agus said.

"Oh my gosh. They have to be okay. Oh please, Lord, let them be okay. Sal, can you drive any faster? Take a right up here," Isabelle directed.

"What happened? How did you find out? Did someone call 911?" Isabelle asked questions in a rapid-fire succession without giving Agus the chance to answer.

"Harriet's neighbor, Madison, called Doug and Alexa at the B&B thinking Harriet might be there. She said flames were shooting out the roof and we needed to come quick. She called 911. I called you but you didn't answer so we stopped on our way to pick you up," Agus said.

What do you know? The chicken lady came through, exactly as Harriet predicted.

Just as Sal, Agus and Isabelle arrived, Harriet was being loaded on a stretcher into an ambulance. Isabelle panicked as she quickly scanned the scene and didn't see the girls anywhere. "Harriet! Harriet," Isabelle screamed, running toward the back of the ambulance.

"Is this your mom?" and EMS technician asked.

"Yes, is she okay?" Isabelle asked. As the EMS technician began to explain, in detail, Isabelle knew she had asked the wrong question. "I'm sorry," she cut him off. "I need to find the girls. Have you seen two pre-teens and a toddler?" Isabelle asked. Just then Agus caught up to Isabelle at the back of the ambulance. "Agus, stay with Harriet. I need to find the girls," Isabelle directed, before immediately running away.

"Grace, Hope, Pinky. Grace, Hope, Pinky..." Isabelle called out, as she dodged among the emergency responders. Police. Fire. Ambulance personnel. *Oh please Lord, let them be okay*. The west side of the house was still on fire. Isabelle had no choice but to run into the burning house. She took a deep breath to fill her lungs with good air and then started to run toward the house. *Ahugg.* She was stopped by a large fireman.

"Ma'am, it's not safe for you to go in there," the fireman said.

"My daughters are in there," she screamed, forcefully trying to shove him aside.

"I can't let you inside," he said, holding her shoulders.

"Let go of me. I need to find my children," she screamed.

The fireman took her shoulders and physically rotated her body. "Are there more than those three with one of our volunteer firefighters?" he asked, pointing toward Grace, her niece Pinky and little Hope, who was cuddled in the arms of a firefighter bent down on one knee. *They're safe.* She could exhale. "That's them. Thank you," she said as she turned to run toward the girls. She was out of breath when she reached the four of them and the volunteer firefighter turned around. *Oh my gosh, not him! Damn.* Pinky and Grace were wrapped in blankets. Owen had Hope tucked warmly and safely into his fireman's coat.

Owen was happy to see her but the sentiment was not returned. "Isabelle. I tried to contact you but your number wouldn't go through," Owen said. There was so much she wanted to say to him. She grabbed Hope out of his arms and held the toddler close to herself. Her angry thoughts were interrupted by one of his colleagues.

"Owen saved your daughter's life," he said.

Obviously she was grateful for this, despite her distain for him. "Sir, you..."

"Teddy. Call me Teddy," the colleague insisted.

"Teddy, are you a volunteer firefighter too?" Isabelle

asked.

"Yes, ma'am," he said.

"I am humbled and grateful that you direct your free time to help save the lives and property of others. And I'm thankful for anyone who does, but," Isabelle started.

"Ma'am, your older girls told Owen the baby was inside and he ran back into the fire to save the baby," Teddy said.

"Is that true?" Isabelle turned and asked Grace. Grace nodded affirmatively. "Grace, Pinky, will you stay with Teddy? I need to talk to Owen," Isabelle said, holding Hope in her arms.

Isabelle started to walk away from the group by about twenty feet. She still had not looked Owen in the eyes or directly acknowledged his presence. He followed her. She held Hope close while she delivered her pointed message. "Thank you for saving Hope. I will be forever grateful to you for that. I will never trust you. I will never like you. I will never be your friend or in your life in any capacity, but I will be eternally grateful to you for saving my child," Isabelle said.

"Wait. Isabelle. What happened? We were good. We kissed. You kissed me back. And a week later when I reached out to you, your phone blocked me. And now you show up here with this indignant demand that I somehow have a tragically flawed character, despite the fact that I ran into a fire to save your daughter's life – which I would have done for anyone, by the way. So please, explain, because right now you sound crazy." Owen laid out his logical conclusion for Isabelle's madness.

"Me crazy? Me crazy? You gave my late husband's ring to your fiancée, and then you worked together to extort me. You lured me to the coffee shop and she tried to sell it to me for five hundred dollars. Seriously? That is the lowest of the low. You deserve nothing from me except a thank you for saving my daughter's life, which I already gave you," Isabelle said. Isabelle unzipped her jacket to show Owen Arnie's ring hanging around her neck.

Owen turned sheet white. Every bit of color drained from his face and neck. This was his worst fear that Isabelle would find out the truth, that he had the ring, before he had a chance to tell her or return it. "Wait. I didn't give it to anyone. What did this woman look like?"

"What does your fiancée look like, Owen? You two-timing bastard. You kissed me while you were engaged to another woman." Isabelle did not express rage very often but when she did, she could break glass. Hope woke up with the ruckus and the sense that her mom was clearly upset. "It's okay, baby, it's okay." She tried to comfort the child.

"Listen please," Owen said. "I don't know what you've been told. I never gave your ring to anyone. I found it in Maui after you left from coffee and I intended to give it to you several times. But I never gave it to anyone. Please believe me. I am not a perfect man, but would never lie to you," Owen said. He paused. "Did she have short red hair and glasses?"

"Yes. And a big rock on her finger, and she said you were her fiancé," Isabelle added.

"When did this happen?" Owen asked, curious to piece together the timeline.

"It doesn't matter. I have Arnie's ring back and that's all I care about."

"Isabelle, when did this happen?" Owen persisted.

"The morning after you kissed me. You texted me to meet you at Utopia. First you stood me up. Then, when I asked you about the ring after your fiancé tried to get money out of me, you told me something came up and asked how I found out about the ring. I felt utterly devastated. How could I open my heart to such a man? That's when I blocked your number," Isabelle said.

"I never texted you to meet me at Utopia," Owen said. "Oh gosh," Owen paused. "Isabelle, the night we kissed, I lost my phone. I remember because I was going to text you to say I had a wonderful time. Jill said she found my phone the next day in the yard." Owen stopped. "I didn't lose it. She took it. Isabelle, believe me. Please. You received incorrect information, in every way. I will deal with this. But for my part. I tried to give you the ring at the restaurant. I wanted to give you the ring when we kissed, but I didn't have it with me. I should have come clean with you immediately. I hated having it between us and I'm sorry. I screwed up. But I never gave your ring to anyone else and I'm not engaged to anyone and I never lied to you. You're angry and that's understandable. I would be too. Please believe me."

Isabelle stood silently for a few seconds, squarely looking at him, not sure what to believe. "I need to make sure the girls are okay and get to the hospital to check on Harriet. I can't do this right now," Isabelle said, before quickly turning in the general direction of Grace, Hope and Pinky. By this time, Richard and Carrie were comforting Pinky and Zach and Amone were with Grace. Liberty huddled close as well.

"Is everything okay?" Zach asked. Isabelle stared off into the night's sky. "Izz? Are you okay?" Zach asked, gently shaking her shoulder.

She looked at him. "We've all be through so much. What else can happen?" Isabelle fell into her brother's broad, firm chest. He pulled her close and kissed the top of her head. She pulled back slightly. "Will you take the girls? I need to get to the hospital. I need to get to Harriet," Isabelle said.

"I need to get Amone home. This isn't good for her out here. Let's get everyone back to the B&B and make a plan from there. It's cold and smoky here and there's nothing we can do but get in the way. I gave the fire chief my number in case he has any follow-up questions," Zach said.

Isabelle was too tired to think through the details at this

point. Once again, Zach stepped in to make Isabelle feel safe.

◆ ◆ ◆

"Hold the elevator," a familiar voice called out just as the doors were shutting with Isabelle inside. When she did, she wished she hadn't.

"Hi," she unenthusiastically said, as Owen stepped inside.

"Perfect timing. I was coming to see you," he said, holding what appeared to be a dusty, possibly antique book.

"You're not going to impress me with poetry or anything else, Professor" she said, glancing down at the book he had tucked between his jacket sleeve and torso.

"It's a good thing, because I haven't prepared anything," he said, laughing as if he cracked himself up with his own joke. "I came to bring this to you," he said, referring to the book, but keeping it just outside her reach until she heard him out. The elevator reached the third floor and Owen waited back to let Isabelle step off first.

"You sure it belongs to you?" she asked snidely. Owen did not take kindly to this comment.

"Okay, I'm going to say this once. When you were misled about me and what I had done, you had every right to think poorly of me. But I told you the truth. I apologized for my part in it. And now I expect you to respond in the courteous and respectful way that I know aligns with who you are. These on-going jabs are beneath you and I expect more from you," he said as he started to hand her the book, and then pulled back as she reached for it. "While I have your attention, I dealt with Jill, as I told you I would. She moved out and I paid her for her legal help on the patent," Owen said.

"So now I'm supposed to run back to your arms?" Isabelle

asked.

"No. Now you're supposed to acknowledge that I kept my word, and when you see me at church or in the community, you'll act civilized and appropriately as the smart, kind woman I know you to be – and not like some schoolgirl holding a grudge. Understood?"

Isabelle did not like in any such way that Owen kept Arnie's ring from her, but she respected how he was handling the situation and her now. She had no choice but to follow his lead, at least on this issue. "Understood," Isabelle said as she nodded affirmatively. "So what is this book you brought me? Something whimsical about fish hatcheries?" she said, the edges of her mouth curling up.

"It looks like a diary. I'm guessing it belongs to your aunt. She had it tucked away for safe-keeping, that's for sure," Owen said.

"Where was it?" Isabelle asked.

"On a crossbeam of a half-destroyed wall. It was sealed inside the walls of her house and I retrieved it during mop-up. It's a little smoky and damp. I thought I better grab it in case the house was demolished. It was surrounded by ash so I'm not even sure how it survived the fire. But it did, so I brought it to you for her. How is she doing?" Owen asked.

"She's still unconscious. They have her on oxygen. Her doctor expects a recovery but with her health history, co-morbidities, and age, nothing is certain," Isabelle said.

"I'll keep her in my prayers," Owen said. "And you."

"Thanks," Isabelle said, accepting the book. "I'll make sure she gets this. I should get to her," Isabelle said. As she started walking down the hall, Owen pressed the button to call the elevator. He watched her walk away, hoping she would at least look back. After the elevator doors opened, closed and whisked Owen away, Isabelle turned and looked back at the empty corridor. She had memories of Arnie walking away and she didn't want this imprint in her mind again, this time with Owen. She closed her eyes.

CHAPTER 12

When Isabelle arrived in Harriet's room, she had a flashback to just over four years prior at Portland Providence. Outside of Harriet's hospital room window, a few stubborn leaves remained on the trees outside – the sturdy ones that defied the infamous Ellensburg wind. Isabelle thumbed through the book Owen delivered to her, just long enough to confirm it was not Harriet's diary, but instead, her mother's diary that Harriet so desperately wanted.

Journal in hand, Isabelle walked over to the window to gaze across the campus before settling into a moderately comfortable, over-sized leather chair to begin reading. *Sealed inside a wall. Just as Arnie foretold,* she thought, as she stared at the first entry, penned in 1973.

At first, Isabelle enjoyed the pure voyeurism of reading any new love story. In fact, she was so engrossed in the story that she momentarily set aside the fact that this was the precious story of how her parents first met. As a teenager, Isabelle longed her ask her mom these questions. And now, here they were. In her mother's voice and her mother's handwriting. The journal started just has Joy had met up with a fellow with whom she seemed to be quite taken. *I wanted to reach up and brush the smudge off his face but couldn't bear to come across inappropriately forward. His hearty laugh drew me in as I hoped he would ask my name. I wasn't even sure if he noticed me. Then in what can only be described as a most incredible vision, I saw us together, running through a field of sunflowers. He was chasing me. I ran jubilantly, as fast as I could, not to get away from him, but to prolong the moment until he caught me and took me in his arms.*

Isabelle stopped reading for a moment as the vision created by the words sunk in. *Isabelle contemplated putting the book down.* She didn't exactly want visions of her parents actually getting together. *Is this why dad sealed the journal in the wall? So no one else would find it? Wow!* Isabelle set the book down on a nearby table.

The suspense was too much. Isabelle couldn't resist picking the book back up. She smiled as she read this the words of this unfolding love story. *This is so romantic! I want to find this. I want someone to chase me through a field of sunflowers.* By this time, she was glued to the book, hanging on every word. *Every woman longs for this.*

When a nurse walked into the room, Isabelle was too engrossed to look up. Even when she spoke to Isabelle, it was as if her words were silent, until they weren't and Isabelle let out a startled yelp.

"Are you okay, ma'am?" the nurse asked.

Isabelle was immersed in the world of 1973 to the point that her attention had fully time-traveled decades back. Isabelle's lack of facial expression and awareness gave the distinct appearance as if she had just suffered a stroke.

"Are you okay? My name is Jennifer and I'm a nurse on this floor. Do I need to call a Rapid Response?" the nurse asked again.

Isabelle could see Jennifer but she couldn't hear her. All that registered were the words on the page in the diary. *"Hi, I'm Jack," the handsome man reached out his hand to shake mine. My voice quivered as our eyes met. I hoped he couldn't sense how nervous I felt or how much I liked him. "Hi Jack. I'm Joy."*

Isabelle gasped and impulsively started sobbing, rocking forward and back ever so slightly. Finally the nurse was able to get her attention. "Are you okay?" Isabelle plastered her hands onto the pages of the book, hoping that if she pressed hard enough, she could actually feel her mother.

Isabelle looked up at the nurse, crying and short of breath. "I'm fine," she finally managed to get out. "I'm fine," she covered her mouth with her hand, looked down at the diary and then back at the nurse. She drank in her mother's beautiful penmanship. "This was my mother's..." Isabelle pressed the book to her chest, again trying to subconsciously feel Joy through her skin into her heart. "This diary belonged to my mother. My whole life I longed to know her. I longed to hear her words. I longed to imagine her life. And all this time, her diary was sealed in the walls of the house where I grew up. It was almost lost in the fire," Isabelle explained to the nurse, shaking her head slowly side-to-side.

"Ma'am, I thought you were having a stroke. I almost called Rapid Response," Jennifer said, in a kind, soft-spoken tone.

By this time, Isabelle had regained her composure. "I suppose if there was a passage that could induce a stroke. this would be it," Isabelle said. "But I'm fine, thank you." All she wanted was for the nurse to leave the room so she could get back to the diary. She knew the time would come to share it with others: Harriet, Grace, Zach. But right now, in this moment and this hospital room, the diary was exclusively hers to devour and digest.

"If you need anything, please ask," Jennifer reiterated. Isabelle smiled and nodded, and the nurse turned her focus to Harriet.

Isabelle had lived the majority of her life somewhat jealous of Zach for being two years older and having two more years with their parents. Even being ten when they died, instead of eight, gave him the advantage of remembering more about their mannerisms, more about household projects and picnics, their mother's garden, and the most mundane activities for which she longed for just a glimpse. And suddenly, as a parent, it hit her how critical it would be for her to make sure her girls never felt this same anguish over missing the common details about Arnie.

Realizing how precious these journal entries were to her, Isabelle vowed to make sure that Grace and Hope always felt safe asking questions about Arnie, regardless of how mundane their curiosity seemed to Isabelle. Although Hope was only three, Isabelle knew a day would come when she would have questions. Arnie mattered to her more than she ever realized when he was alive and she knew his legacy would one day help shape how their girls viewed the world and themselves.

Harriet caught Isabelle's attention when she moved her hand. *Is she regaining consciousness?* "Harriet? It's me Isabelle. I'm here." She stood up quickly and rushed to Harriet's side. Setting the diary down on the nightstand next to her bed, Isabelle took Harriet's hands in her own. "Harriet?" Isabelle whispered softly, inches from Harriet's face. She watched her aunt intently, but there was no visible response. She sighed with disappointment, just as Carrie entered the room.

"How's she doing?" Carrie asked. It was strange to see Carrie in an hospital environment but not wearing scrubs.

"Same. I thought she was waking up but it doesn't seem to be the case," Isabelle said.

"Harriet awoke earlier. Didn't the nurses tell you?" Carrie asked.

"No," Isabelle said, in an agitated tone. "Why did she lose consciousness again?"

"She's heavily sedated so her body can rest but she's going to be fine," Carrie assured.

"Oh, what a relief! Why do they tell you and not me? It's not like you practice at this hospital or even in this state." The harsh words had escaped Isabelle's mouth before she caught herself and realized she was being unfairly jealous and possessive. "I'm sorry. I didn't mean that. I don't know why I said that."

"It's fine. I introduced myself as a physician at Portland Providence. Of course, I thought they briefed you," Carrie said.

Isabelle chuckled. "Of course you did. I really am sorry. I totally over-reacted." Isabelle tipped her head down to Carrie's shoulder. Just then Isabelle's phone rang, so she hustled across the room to pick it up. It was her literary agent. "Just a second, Donna. Hey Carrie, I'm going to take this. I'll be back," Isabelle said as she stepped out of the room.

Just as Isabelle returned to the doorway, her eyes immediately found the diary on the table. *Drats!* And then suddenly, she was bathed in relief. Harriet was awake and talking to Carrie. Isabelle felt torn; she was happy Harriet was alert, very happy. But she wasn't yet ready to share the diary. She hadn't finished reading it. In fact, she had barely opened it. She stood just outside the doorway trying to think of how to retrieve the book without prompting any questions. She could overhear the conversation between Harriet and Carrie. *I've always wondered what they talked about?* And so, she stood there perfectly still, evesdropping.

"Richard asked me to marry him?" Carrie gushed. "I said yes and I'm moving to Maui the first of the year." Carrie's voice was happy, and hearing this made Isabelle smile.

"You know he will let you down," Harriet said. Hearing this made Isabelle wrinkle her nose. *Harriet, what is wrong with you? Be happy for her. Congratulate her!*

"Because he's a man?" Carrie asked.

"No darling, because he's human. And you will let him down. Because you're human. It's how you recover from disagreements that will determine if your relationship can stand the test of time. We all enter romantic relationships with the fantasy that this magical other person who makes us feel fireworks when we kiss is going to somehow make everything that happens in life absolutely wonderful, and it's simply not true. It's a monumental lie. And it's a lot of pressure to put on another person, especially someone we claim to love," Harriet said.

"Well, I don't have any illusions about him. I know he has PTSD and I know what happened to him in the Army. It's probably something that will always be there, but it's something we're committed to handling together," Carrie said.

"Do you want to talk about it?" Harriet asked. *Oh Harriet, you didn't just say that*, Isabelle thought. Isabelle leaned in a few inches to hear Carrie's response.

"No, it's a private matter that he felt I deserved to know; I gave him my word that I would never tell a soul," Carrie said. *I wonder if it's what came between him and Arnie? Not that it matters now.*

"You know what I learned being married to Frank?" Harriet asked Carrie. Instead of verbally responding, Carrie paused for Harriet to continue. "I learned that love is not a feeling. If it's a feeling, you can fall out of love as quickly as you fall in love. Attraction is a feeling. Sexual chemistry is a feeling. But love is a choice. Love is there after their looks fade, their jokes are stale, they fart in bed, and their health declines. Love is the commitment you make to be vulnerable when it's scary and honest when it would be so much easier to lie or just leave out enough key details to avoid a confrontation. If you can promise him those things, and he can promise them to you, you can work through anything," Harriet said.

Wow! That was beautiful, Harriet. But why didn't Carrie get the religion lectures you always save for me? Isabelle knew the answer to her own question. While faith was very important to Harriet, she loved Carrie for who she was. Somehow Harriet knew that Carrie would listen to only so much, and so she boiled down her advice, seasoning it just so, to meet the needs of Carrie's palate. Every time Isabelle came close to believing a stereotype about Harriet, her aunt surprised her in the best possible way.

A floor nurse was walking toward her so she held her phone back to her ear hoping it would prevent the nurse from asking if she needed anything. It worked. The nurse walked on by.

"I love you, Harriet," Carrie said. "Whether it's a marriage, a friendship or a sibling relationship, I think for me, love comes down to four things: loyalty, communication, hope in the future, and faith in each other, at least to the level the relationship warrants. What I have with Richard is not perfect but it is real. We can depend on each other. It works for us."

Eves-dropping left Isabelle with more questions than answers. And while the curious part of her wanted to dig for answers, the mature part of her decided to move on. *Izz, it's not your business. Whatever transpired between Arnie and Richard was between them, and that's where it should stay.*

The nurse who walked by a few minutes before was headed back toward Harriet's room, and Grace, Pinky and Richard were steps behind her. Isabelle made gestures as if she had been on the phone the whole time and was just hanging up.

"Hi mom," Grace said, as she and Pinky casually walked into Harriet's room and sat down. Richard acknowledged Isabelle with a nod and then greeted Carrie in the hospital room with a quick peck.

As Isabelle entered the room, Carrie slid her left hand into her pocket to hide her ring. Isabelle pretended to not notice. "Are you good with us leaving the girls with you?" Carrie asked.

"Of course," Isabelle responded. *That's a weird question.*

Why wouldn't I be?

"Isabelle, would you mind walking out with us? There's something I wanted to talk to you about," Carrie asked.

Isabelle felt overjoyed. Finally, after all these years, Carrie is going to confide in me about her wedding before she tells the whole family – just like a real sister would do. "Absolutely," Isabelle said, again leaving the room, with the diary still on the nightstand beside Harriet's bed.

Walking down the hall, Carrie started. "I want to thank you for sharing Harriet with me for all these years. I know she was your surrogate mom, but after my mom died, you shared her with me and she became my surrogate mom too, and I appreciate it."

"Well, we are like sisters, and maybe will be formally, if you and Richard continue dating or you never know." Isabelle wanted to set Carrie up to share her big news without letting on that she overheard her tell Harriet. "I mean, have you two thought about it?"

Richard cleared his throat. Carrie stopped and turned to face him, leaving Isabelle as clearly an awkward third wheel. After a brief standoff, he sighed and nodded. Carrie turned back to Isabelle. "So please don't say anything. We're planning to tell the rest of the family at Thanksgiving, but Richard and I are contemplating sharing a state," Carrie said with excitement. Isabelle tried to hide that she knew they planned to share more than a state.

"Is Richard moving to Portland or are you applying to Queen's Hospital?" Isabelle asked.

"We'll see," Carrie said. Isabelle couldn't help but feel let down by Carrie's lack of transparency. "Okay, well, we'll see you back at the B&B," Carrie said, leaning in to air kiss Isabelle on the cheek.

As momentarily let down as Isabelle felt, she was able to quickly garner perspective through self-talk. *Izz, obviously Richard did not want her to share their news yet. She looked to him for permission and made a decision to compromise. You can't fault her for acquiescing to her soon-to-be-husband. Relationships require compromise and she was showing him that he was her priority. You can't fault her for that. You know you'd do the same thing.* Isabelle took a deep breath in and arrived at Harriet's doorway just in time to hear her dishing out more advice – this time to Grace. Isabelle took a step back so as not to be noticed or intrude.

"Honey, I'm going to tell you something I should have told your mama years ago. That voice inside that guides you – listen to it. Your Grandma Joy once told me that someday I would raise her babies. Yes, she told me that. I tried to push her off. I told her no. But she said she knew it and she said there wasn't anyone in this world she would rather have co-parent Zach and Isabelle," Harriet said.

Isabelle couldn't believe what she was hearing. *What? And you never told me this?*

"Your Grandma Joy had a gift. She saw things and knew things, and that was frightening for me. I didn't know where she got her information. But instead of embracing it and her, I let fear win. You mom has this same gift. And maybe the reason I've always been so hard on her was because I didn't want to lose her too soon the way I lost Joy. I thought if I steered her to a more conventional path I could keep her safe," Harriet said.

"I don't say this to make you sad. I say this to empower you – to support you in listening to your inner voice. Because Grace, you have this gift too." Harriet paused and stared out the window at the half barren trees with only the strong straggler leaves left behind. Pinky sat in a chair in the corner, absorbed in her phone and not paying any attention to the important conversation taking place a few yards from her.

Isabelle wanted to step in, but even more, she needed to

hear the rest of what Harriet would say.

"When we were in Maui, you had a nightmare that I was in a fire," Harriet said. Overhearing this, Isabelle covered her mouth to prevent Harriet and Grace from hearing her gasp. *That's right. Harriet was in a fire. Looking for a book. The Diary. She was looking for the diary. Grace dreamed that, months before it happened. I have to speak up.*

"And in your dream, I was looking for a book. Do you remember that?" Harriet asked.

"I remember having a bad dream and mom telling me it would be okay," Grace said.

"Honey, you asked why I am sad. You asked why I have tears in my eyes. It's because I did something I never believed in and never allowed myself to do before. And I thought it would turn out amazing and it didn't, and now I am mourning a dream," Harriet said.

"Are you mad you did it?" Grace asked.

"No. No, I'm not mad. I'm sad it didn't work out the way I hoped, the way I planned. But not for a second do I regret moving to Ellensburg to connect in some way with Joy."

"What made you sad?" Grace asked. Isabelle loved her daughter's tender heart and inquisitive mind. *She's so spectacular. Isn't she just so spectacular?*

"I moved to Ellensburg, looking for something that I thought would bring me closer to my sister. The truth is that it was the only time my entire life I listened to my intuition and not only listened but took this huge leap of faith to jump into the unknown. I never knew exactly what I was looking for, but I knew there was something meant for me to find. Maybe it was a book, like you dreamed. Maybe it was something else. We'll never know now. The house is a total loss. But do you know what matters more?" Harriet asked Grace.

"What?"

"What matters more is that I honored my sister by listening to my gut, and she would have been so proud of me," Harriet said. "And that journey brought me closer to her than any physical object ever could." Harriet pulled Grace's hands to her lips and kissed them. "My precious Grace, embrace who you are. Listen to your heart always, and so long as your heart is pure, trust the messages you hear," Harriet said.

Upon hearing this, Isabelle knew the moment had come for her to take one of the most unselfish steps she had ever taken in her life. What she was about to do went against her normal inclination. It was that moment she would prove she had become the woman she always wanted to be. With tears flowing down her face, she stepped into the room and walked swiftly to Harriet's bedside. She took Harriet's hand in her right hand and reached across the bed to take Grace's right hand in her left.

"I have never been more proud of you Harriet," Isabelle started, which made the normally stoic Harriet bristle just slightly. "Grace, your dream was real. Harriet, you moved to Ellensburg and when the girls were safe, you went back into the fire because you knew something so special and precious was in there – something no amount of money or reconstruction could ever replace," Isabelle said. Harriet's body relaxed as she gazed her full attention on every word Isabelle shared.

"All is not lost. Mom would have been thrilled and honored to know you listened to your gut. She is proud of you. I am proud of you." Isabelle dropped Harriet's hand to reach to the right and pick up Joy's diary from the nightstand next to Harriet's bed. "The house is a total loss, but there is good news. When the fire department was handling mop-up, Owen found what you were looking for, Harriet. It's mom's diary." Before Isabelle could finish what she was saying, Harriet reached for it and took it from Isabelle's hand, without the slightest bit of frailty. Isabelle continued. "I started reading it and I'd like to finish it when you're done. She was your sister before she was my mom, so it's only fair you get to finish it first," Isabelle said.

Harriet poured her full focus and breath into the diary. She caressed the cover and inhaled the smoky pages as if they offered her the life-saving oxygen she needed to survive. She closed the book, held it to her heart, and began sob. "Joy, oh Joy. Oh Joy," she whimpered softly.

Isabelle never loved Harriet as much as she did in that moment. It felt to her as if the woman who raised her channeled the woman who birthed her and somehow the sisters had merged and become one person with a common goal and shared heart. It was in that exact moment Isabelle realized that the three of them would be forever inseparably bound. Life would always be divided into two parts – life before the fire that led to the diary being found, and then after. Isabelle was hungry to read the rest of her mother's story.

Grace leaned down and laid her head on the side of Harriet's bed, not looking at either women, just staring at a cotton ball that had somehow fallen on the floor. Unceremoniously, the past, present and future of these three women silently and indelibly met and merged, perfectly weaving each thread into a flawless fabric.

Isabelle glanced over at Pinky, still playing on her phone, and at least appearing completely oblivious to the emotional firestorm engulfing the room.

Nurse Jennifer was back, rolling a rover into Harriet's room, to take her blood pressure, oxygen and temperature. "Good news. Your vitals are good and I just heard you're getting discharged today, just in time for Thanksgiving," Jennifer said. She continued to take Harriet's vitals while she made conversation.

"Every year I'm reminded how much I have to be thankful for," Harriet said. Her cheeks were moist from having just wiped her tears away.

"Are you in pain?" Jennifer asked Harriet. "You look like you've been crying."

"Tears of joy. Absolutely tears of joy," Harriet said.

"Well, you clearly have a large and loving family. I wish you all a wonderful Thanksgiving," the sweet nurse said, as she wrapped up.

"Happy Thanksgiving," Harriet responded, as Jennifer moved the rover back toward the door, leaving as quickly as she entered.

Once again, Harriet opened the book and silently started to read, smiling just as Isabelle had when she read the same passage of the day her parents met. Out of generosity, not selfishness, Isabelle would always keep a key piece of information to herself. She vowed never to tell Harriet where the book was recovered, or that it included a letter from her dad to her mom, describing why he paid to have it sealed in the wall when they were on their honeymoon.

Ironically, Jack's motivation for silencing his soon-to-be-wife's visions and dreams was not that unlike Harriet's. Fear. He was afraid someone might think she was crazy or had taken up with questionable spirits. *Oh, daddy, if only you could have known. If only you could have trusted yourself enough to listen to your voice inside as well.* Isabelle didn't judge her dad; she knew he could only make decisions based on the information he had. She also knew Harriet would never have tolerated Jack's actions to keep any part of Joy from her, and if she ever learned that Jack hid the diary, and sealed it in a wall, she would have carried a grudge against him to her own grave. *There's been enough pain. It's time to trust the magic of new beginnings.* For Isabelle, over the course of her struggles, she had come to the conclusion what was right for her: *Life does not need to make sense. True peace comes in trusting that God works all things for our higher good.*

CHAPTER 13

I sabelle drove back to the bed and breakfast with Harriet, Grace and Pinky amidst a farmhouse brimming with family noise and holiday excitement – laughter, random screams and micro conversations yelled out across the kitchen – a cacophony of chatter from multiple conversations being carried on simultaneously in the same room.

It was the holiday setting she had envisioned in her mind's eye for decades and the pinnacle of what she longed for as a child, and hoped for when she met Arnie. It was a perfect blend of noise, hugs, and welcoming greetings of family, and friends who had become like family over the past four years.

It had been an unimaginably difficult past four years, but those years were in the past, and now Isabelle could breathe, laugh, and enjoy the harvest bounty.

Per state laws for bed and breakfast establishments in Washington, Doug and Alexa could not run the kitchen as a business beyond providing breakfast for paying guests. So everyone collectively decided that Thanksgiving would be an *all hands on deck* experience with everyone prepping and cooking Thanksgiving dinner together. Isabelle insisted that Doug and Alexa sit back and let their unofficial guests treat them to an indelible holiday feast – aside from answering questions about where specific pans and kitchen utensils could be found.

Isabelle created a comfortable spot a few feet from the stove for Harriet to relax, in accordance with her doctor's orders, while allowing her to still be a part of the action.

Zach was snapping the ends off the beans with Amone glancing over to periodically infuse familiar spousal direction. Carrie was cleaning and prepping the bird to go into the oven the next day. Agus and her daughter, Olivia, whose sister Alexa and Doug owned the bed and breakfast, peeled potatoes as Salvador recounted his redundant and yet still entertaining stories. Isabelle had heard his stories multiple times in her years working for him at the insurance company. Hearing these familiar tales after her time away from him made her smile and brought back memories of events and people who seemed far more important in the moment than most of them turned out to be.

Isabelle exchanged glances with Agus, who gave her that knowing look that can only come from someone else who has heard the same stories and could even deliver the punch-lines in the same exact tone. "Grace. Pinky. Who wants to help make the pies?" Isabelle called upstairs.

Liberty opened a couple bottles of a Bordeaux blend and Syrah from one of her favorite Eastern Washington vineyards. She discovered the wine after the owner, an orthopedic surgeon, repaired her meniscus after a skiing injury years before.

Isabelle had started rolling out the gluten-free dough for the pies when Agus came up behind her. "Thank you," the stately woman whispered. "Oh what an indelible gift this is," she said. "You know what I've learned?" Agus asked.

"Hopefully how to make a better pie crust than I am," Isabelle joked.

"I've learned that despite the hardships, and despite the plans we have that careen off-course, the human spirit is strong and the divine is woven into the details," Agus said.

Isabelle gently sighed and nodded. "Yes, you may be right."

"Everyone in this room has suffered unimaginable loss. Our family lost a son. And when that happened, we stopped living. Losing a child permanently alters the course of your life. You lost your husband. Your girls lost a dad. Richard and Pinky lost a brother and uncle. You and Zach lost your parents. Harriet lost her only sister. Carrie and Liberty both lost their moms, maybe their dad's I don't know. Amone lost her parents. Every person in this house tonight has lost an immediate family member. And yet, here we are, together, not alone, celebrating life, not mourning another year that has passed. And do you know who every single person in this room is connected to?" Agus paused. Isabelle stopped rolling out the dough and stood before the beautiful lady she so admired, speechless.

Agus continued. "You, Isabelle. You look at your life and it didn't turn out the way you planned. It didn't turn out the way you hoped or ever would have written. But you were the thread that ultimately sewed this fabric together. So thank you. Thank you for showing up and inviting us to join you on this journey. Thank you for including me in your kindness project. That was the first step I took in healing from Tim's death. Thank you for holding on when it would have been so much easier to give up. Your tiny, flickering candle lit the way to fill this whole room with light."

By the time Agus finished speaking, the kitchen had grown silent. Liberty had moved closer and boldly asked, "What happened to your son? What happened to Tim?" It wasn't an evening for holding anything back.

"He was killed in a car accident on Christmas Eve, twelve years ago. I insisted he come for Christmas Eve services. Olivia and Alexa were in town and I had spent weeks perfectly preparing the house. He wanted to come the next morning but I convinced him to arrive for dinner and midnight mass," Agus shared.

Sal had made his way behind her and placed his hand on her shoulder. "Honey, don't do this to yourself. It was an accident. No one could have known," Sal said.

Instead of brushing him away, as she often had in the past, she returned his embrace. "It was a snowy Christmas Eve night, and he ended up in a little critical care access hospital in White Salmon, Washington. We rushed to get to him but we arrived too late," Agus said.

"Skyline Hospital," Liberty said.

"What?" Isabelle asked.

"Skyline Hospital. In White Salmon, Washington. My mom was a nurse there," Liberty said.

"Yes, that was the place," Agus said.

Being a veterinarian, Liberty was used to comforting human parents of beloved animals. Instinctively, she set her glass of wine down on a counter and walked over to Sal and Agus to provide comfort. "My mom, Evelyn, was a nurse in the ICU at Skyline Hospital on Christmas Eve, twelve years ago. It was a snowy night when a young man, headed to a Christmas party hit a deer on 84 and was rushed by ambulance to her ER. She felt such a connection to him, that after he was stabilized, she asked to go with him to the ICU. It was out of the ordinary, even for her. Nurses are assigned departments or floors. But that night, she was his nurse. I remember mom telling me the story and how much of an impact this young man had on her."

"Tim hit a deer," Agus mouthed to Sal. "Tim's car hit a deer the night he died."

"Mom stayed with him, and talked to him, she told me. She didn't know if he had any specific beliefs, so being that it was Christmas Eve, she read him the Christmas story from Luke two," Liberty shared.

"It was twelve years ago, for sure?" Agus asked.

"Yes. I know that because I was asked to cover a shift at an emergency pet clinic and I told her I was sorry I would miss the cake for Baby Jesus and the Christmas story that year. Later, she said it was meant to be. She pick up an ER shift that night and told me she read the Christmas story to her patient to bring him peace," Liberty spoke softly, her voice filled with great sincerity.

"What else can you tell us?" Agus asked, hanging on every word the veterinarian spoke. "What can you tell us about that night? About Tim?"

Isabelle reached for a tissue and handed it to Agus, who clearly needed more than the edge of her sleeve by this time. And then she reached for a second one for herself.

"I'm sorry. I wish I had more to tell you. I was young and busy and wasn't paying as much attention as I would have, if only I had known that would be my mom's last Christmas too," Liberty said, starting to sniffle. "But I can tell you this: Evelyn was one of the kindest, most tender people I have ever known my entire life. It was she, who instilled in me, my sense of compassion for the animals I treat, and their owners in need of understanding and care. There could never be another human or nurse better trained or equipped to escort your son from this life to the next. I hope when it's my time, her spirit returns to walk with me," Liberty said. By this time, the veterinarian had fully regained her composure. Dealing with sickness and even death in her emergency pet clinic, Liberty was accustomed to managing stress with grace.

Isabelle suddenly realized something amazing. Whether she would receive outside confirmation or not wouldn't matter, but all the pieces were coming together. The man on the bench. The woman carrying the boxes. Snoopy getting hurt and Isabelle taking him to Liberty's clinic. Agus and Sal. The Kindness Project. They were all connected. The last four years did not happen by accident. They were all threads within a greater design. Isabelle was the connection to bring peace, closure and new beginnings to two families still shredded by mourning more than a decade later. She knew in that moment, she was chosen. Every trial she endured led her to this moment and enabled her to bring this special and eclectic group of precious friends together for healing on this unforgettable Thanksgiving Eve.

"Agus," Isabelle said. "Agus, do you have a picture of Tim?"

"Not with me. I'll show you sometime at the house," Agus said.

"I have albums upstairs," said Alexa, who had already stepped out of the room to grab one before Isabelle could even turn around.

Isabelle returned to the counter and the pie dough, which had started to dry out. It wasn't rolling very well and she wasn't sure if she should add water or milk, so without missing a beat, she looked over to the one person she had confidence would know. "Harriet, it's dried out. What should I add to soften it up?"

Standing up to walk over and inspect it more carefully, Harriet didn't hesitate in her assessment. "Start over, dear. A poor crust will detract from the look and taste of your pies, and you don't want that. Not on Thanksgiving," Harriet said.

Isabelle couldn't help but smile. Oh how she had come to love this woman and the solidarity of her convictions, whether about current events or pie crusts. So many things ran through Isabelle's mind, but all that came out were two words, "Sounds good." This was really all that Harriet wanted to hear as well.

Alexa returned with a short stack of photo albums, and was instantly surrounded by her sister Olivia, Agus, Sal and Doug. They poured through the pictures and smiled. "Oh remember that car?" was the first of many reminiscent stories the family told each other about good times that had been hidden far away. Liberty cozied up to peek at the young patient who touched her mom's heart, as Carrie and Richard also looked at pictures and asked questions.

Doug made his way over to the sink for a glass of water, next to where Isabelle was once again rolling out pie crusts. "You know, we weren't allowed to ever speak his name," Doug quietly mentioned to Isabelle. "This Thanksgiving really is something very special."

Isabelle poured the buttery pecan mixture into one shell and stirred the apples, sugar and cinnamon together for a second pie. "You're making a pumpkin pie, right?" Harriet asked.

"Do you think we need three pies?" Isabelle asked. Immediately she knew the answer before Harriet answered. Harriet would never make a suggestion for something she didn't feel was important. *Of course she thinks we need three pies.*

"Honey, we need a pumpkin pie for Thanksgiving. It's tradition," Harriet said.

"Yes, of course. You're right." These five words saved Isabelle a great many headaches and arguments the last few years.

The front porch doorbell rang, causing everyone to stop and look around with surprised and questioning faces. "Are we expecting anyone?" Olivia asked.

"I'll see who's there," Doug said, as he left the kitchen. He returned a minute later with a man behind a large potted burgundy chrysanthemum with a shiny yellow bow. When he moved the mum aside, Isabelle looked up from setting the pumpkin pie in the oven and smiled. *You really think flowers are going to win me over, Professor?*

"Harriet, I heard you were released and these are for you," Owen said, walking past Isabelle and over to where Harriet was sitting."

"Oh they're beautiful. Thank you, Owen," Harriet said.

"How are you feeling ma'am?" Owen asked.

"Just fine," she said, before covering her mouth for a small cough. "It takes more than a devastating fire to keep me down," Harriet said.

They are some pair, Isabelle laughed to herself glancing over at the two of them. She hadn't completely forgiven Owen for the ring incident, but it wasn't in her nature to carry a grudge. *It's Thanksgiving. I guess if there's ever a time to let something go it's this week.*

When Owen was finished buttering up to Harriet, he came over to where Isabelle was finalizing her design on an apple pie. "That looks awesome. Apple?" Owen asked.

"Yes, Sir," Isabelle playfully replied.

"Apple's my favorite. I look forward to sinking my teeth into it," Owen said.

"Really? That's a bold prediction." Isabelle challenged.

"Harriet invited me for Thanksgiving dinner tomorrow," Owen said, pleased with himself.

"Well then, I guess I'll see you for Thanksgiving, Professor."

"How about you walk me out?" Owen suggested.

It wasn't something Isabelle wanted to do, but she couldn't think of a way to decline. "Give me a minute. I'm just about done here," she said, finishing the last touches before sliding the pie into the lower oven.

She grabbed a random coat from the coat rack by the front door. It wasn't hers but she didn't care. When they got outside Owen turned to face her.

"I hope you're not going to kiss me again," she said. "Don't fool yourself into thinking it's that easy to get back into my good graces," she said. Although her tone was flirtatious, she wasn't really kidding.

"Isabelle, I wish we could go back to the day we met in Maui, or even the day you were stranded on the side of the road. I would do everything different. I just want you to know that," Owen said.

"Please don't ask for a second chance right now," she said.

"I just wanted to tell you that I'm sorry. I wish life had a do-over button. It doesn't. I know that. I just didn't want you to think that I believed that flowers for your aunt or a few laughs made everything okay. But I really am sorry," he said.

Isabelle respected anyone willing to own a mistake and apologize. "Thanks." She sighed loudly. "I, I mean that. Thanks." She reached her hand out to shake his hand, only to have him tip his head to the side and shrug with his arms out for a hug. So she accommodated. She gave him a courtesy hug and then quickly pulled back. "I'll see you tomorrow," she said, with a smile.

"Tomorrow," he said, smiling and then turned to walk twenty or so steps to his car. He waved as he opened the car door; she turned to step back inside.

The next morning, Isabelle crept down the stairs, toward the kitchen on the first floor, before anyone else was up. She paused as memories flooded her mind. She remembered taking these same steps at her grandparents' house as a child. She paused half way down the staircase just to take it in. Suddenly, she did something that even surprised her. She sat down on the stairs, putting her head just below where it would have been the last time she visited this house. She was eight years old. Her parents had recently died in a car accident, and she and Zach stayed with their grandparents before Frank and Harriet moved them to Portland.

The comforting smells of baked pies lingered in the air from the night before, just as they did when she was small. As her mind took a trip back in time, she could hear a young Harriet and Grandma Mae, catching up on whatever was top news in Ellensburg that week. Hearing them giggle and share sweet stories of Joy and their love for her, made Isabelle curious what it must be like to be an adult. As a child, she felt comforted by overhearing them comfort each other. It sounded so different from half way up the staircase.

Snapping back to the present day, Isabelle smiled when she noticed that the same coat rack that stood by the front door years ago, still stood there today. The coat rack from which she grabbed an overcoat the night before when she stepped outside to talk to Owen. *Funny the prior owners never moved that.*

Not everything was the same. She looked up at the walls which had been painted a trendy cocoa color, unlike the white walls of her youth. And of course Isabelle was no longer the same. She was no longer scared. She was no longer insecure. She was no longer sad or angry. The last few years had transformed her into a kind, vivacious, confident woman – the woman she always knew was inside.

Over the past four years, she had released Arnie, released Masingho and while she hadn't closed the door on Owen, she held no expectations of any future, existent or nonexistent, with him. She was a biological daughter to Jack and Joy, a daughter of love and circumstance to Frank and Harriet, a sister to Zach, Amone, Richard and Carrie. She was a mom to Grace and Hope and she was a friend to herself and others. Her life was rich and full, despite the fact that it looked nothing like the vision she held in her mind when she was young. She no longer lamented lost dreams, but rather sat on the stairs of the old farmhouse fully embracing and grateful for the people and blessings that surrounded her in that moment.

After taking this all in, and gently embracing the stark message from Agus the night before – *everyone here has lost someone significant* – Isabelle vowed in that moment that no matter what lied ahead, she would live life fully, embracing the victories and obstacles as they came. She would love and laugh. She would breathe and cry, and most of all, she would forgive. She would forgive others and she would forgive herself.

And with that, she stood back up and walked to the kitchen to start coffee. With the morning sun pouring in the east-facing windows, a chill in the air and the familiar aroma of coffee brewing, she looked at the small stack of photo albums brought downstairs the night before. She anticipated opening the pages, knowing exactly who she would find. As much as she initially wanted to rush over last night, she wanted more to hold this moment sacred in her own heart. With no one else in the house yet awake, she walked purposefully over to the albums.

"Tim." Isabelle spoke his name aloud softly. She opened the top album and began to thumb carefully through the pages, until she landed on a picture that looked exactly like the man who had changed her life. It was Tim who saved her from herself, and in return, she would knit his family back together.

Tim was the man on the bench who sat there, day and night, for weeks until she answered the call to help, hours before Snoopy needed critical medical care. The night that Dr. Liberty Sloop took care of her dog, and listened to the promptings from her own angel to discount the bill in the exact amount Isabelle spent on food for the then nameless man on the bench.

Isabelle bent down close to the album, to get a perfect look at his face. She looked at his eyes. And she remembered the only words he spoke. *Thank you.* Isabelle placed her finger on his photo and looked up, as if to greet him in the sky. *No Tim. Thank you. Thank you for getting my attention and changing my life.*

Isabelle could finally, without provocation, breathe in deeply and exhale fully and appreciate her entire body, heart and soul filled with peace.

Just as the coffeemaker beeped to indicate the coffee was ready, Isabelle began to hear creaking on the floor above. She would not have much more time alone, but the time she had was enough. She looked at the photo of Tim one more time, smiled, and gently closed the book.

As she poured her first cup of coffee, the kitchen slowly started to fill with her beautiful patchwork family, awaking and gathering to celebrate their first Thanksgiving together. "I hope you like it strong," she told Carrie, referring to the coffee.

"It's the only way I make it through 12-hour shifts at the hospital sometimes," Carrie replied. Soon the farmhouse kitchen was filled with adults and kids alike.

"Who wants to help me make Swedish pancakes?" Harriet asked Grace and Pinky. Both girls immediately jumped on board, reaching for the sugar, butter, and plates to start the assembly line, as Harriet whipped together the sweet fluffy batter.

"My mom had the best vanilla peach topping recipe she used to make," said Liberty. "I watched her make it enough; I'm sure I can recreate it."

"Do we have whipped cream or ice cream?" Amone asked.

"It's Thanksgiving. We have everything, if not upstairs then try the refrigerator downstairs," Alexa said.

Isabelle smiled as she looked back at the bustling kitchen before heading upstairs to shower. Finally, her life was filled with love. She had the big, crazy, eclectic family she always wanted, always prayed for and would treasure as long as she lived.

◆ ◆ ◆

Everyone was present, and most seated at the table, when Zach proudly carried in the ornately-dressed, golden-brown turkey. The long table was exquisitely decorated with ribbons, candles, miniature pumpkins and far too much food for one sitting. Amone was steps behind Zach with the carving knife and meat fork. Isabelle was pretty sure most Thanksgiving restaurant buffets didn't have the menu variety served up this day.

"Before Zach carves the turkey and we all enjoy this marvelous bounty together, I'd like to ask each of you to join me in sharing something you feel grateful for today, and I will close with a word of grace," Harriet said. It really was more of a determination than a request, but everyone went along with it graciously. Turning to Doug, seated at her right, Harriet said, "Would you be so kind as to start us off?"

Not one to bring attention to himself, Doug seemed a bit surprised to be put on the spot, but after barely more than a beat, he rolled with it. He looked at his wife, Alexa, as he spoke. "I'm thankful to open this bed and breakfast with my wife. It's been our dream and Sal and Agus made it possible. And to meet all of you and that all of you could spend this very special Thanksgiving with us," Doug said.

"I want to pinch myself every day that I wake up to Doug and Judy, and especially now in this amazing home," Alexa started. Judy was sitting in a highchair between Doug and Alexa. "Being a wife and a mom has made my heart happier than I thought anything ever could. I don't know what they're talking about when they say terrible twos. Judy is my daily dream come true. And how great now that she will grow up with Hope," Alexa said.

Alexa's sister was next. "Almost twelve years ago our family was shattered. I'm thankful that last night you all helped us put the pieces back together. We spent far too long in our own corners trying to cope," Olivia said. Olivia reached for her dad's hand beside her, and squeezed it to let him know it was his turn.

Isabelle's former boss was brief – completely unlike his stories that seemed to have no end. "I'm thankful for second chances. It turns out I really enjoy retirement. Who knew?" Sal said, with a laugh.

"The last twenty-four hours of having our family back together, including the memory of Tim, and combining that with all of you, who we will always love like family," Agus stopped speaking and just started nodding. She quickly regained her composure and continued. "Isabelle, Sal had many dear employees throughout the years. None of them will ever mean what you do. Grace, I'll never forget when you invited me to join you and your mom in sharing gifts with people who do not have permanent homes. Your little kindness project touched me as much as the people you set out to help. You are a special young lady with a great big heart, and I am ever so honored you included me," Agus said.

Liberty was next. "I became a veterinarian because my mom was a nurse and she showed me, by the way she lived, how to care for others through genuine empathy. I bought the emergency pet clinic in some ways to hide. My staff and I work every weekend, every night, and every holiday. I still can't believe I agreed to join your family this weekend. But honestly, what a miracle this has been. Isabelle, I thought it was crazy when my mom's voice in my head told me to discount your bill by an additional nineteen dollars. And I thought it was crazy when you said you knew my mom. But it was no accident that you needed my clinic that night," Liberty said. Then, physically turning her body to face the part of the table where Tim's family sat, she continued. "Sharing mom's story of caring for your son and brother, seemed like a gift for you. But it was equally a gift for me. It reminded me of who she was and who I strive to be.

All these strange coincidences were no mistake. Our paths were mean to converge here. And so, I'm thankful that I listened when I could have said no – but my heart – said yes," Liberty said.

While the expressions of gratitude were heartfelt and cathartic, Isabelle hoped she could count on Grace to lighten things up. "I'm thankful that Yia Yia is home safe, and that we all got out of the fire. I'm thankful that Pinky and Uncle Richard could come from Hawaii. I'm thankful that my mom is happy again and she makes me feel safe. And I'm thankful for mashed potatoes with butter, which we never get at home because mom says they have too many complex carbohydrates," Grace said.

"Nice," Isabelle chimed in, and everyone else welcomed a moment to laugh.

"I'm thankful that this amazing woman agreed to be my wife. Yes! We're getting married so you'll all be invited to pack your bags for Hawaii!" Richard said. And then turning to Carrie, he added, "You know my flaws, my weaknesses, my temper, my fears and none of them scare you. I can't wait to spend the rest of my life with you."

"To Richard and Carrie," Zach cheered, raising his wine glass, setting off a group toast in the middle of the gratitude sharing.

"And I'm thankful to be moving to Hawaii, and never shoveling snow or stomping through cold rain again," Carrie said.

"Oh we get rain. Don't fool yourself," Pinky said. "But it's not cold. I'm thankful to be here. It turns out Ellensburg is way more fun than I thought it would be because I get to spend time with my cousin. Although the fire was terrifying. But we lived."

"After a year of IVF, mood swings, crazy hormones and this guy driving me seriously nuts, I'm thankful that we will be bound to each other for life, not just as husband and wife, but also as parents," Amone paused and then shouted, "We're having a baby!"

"What?!" Isabelle gasped, with joy.

"I made her keep it a secret," Zach said. "You can hurt me later," he added, teasingly.

"Well, it's a great secret. Hey, I wondered why you didn't drink any wine last night. I count on you to finish off the bottle with me," Isabelle joked, then raising her glass added, "Congratulations!"

Never the smooth one, Zach did not disappoint. "I'm thankful for all of you," Zach said generally. "And even you," he said jokingly, pointing to his sister. "And especially you," he said to Amone, leaning in for a peck on the lips.

It was Isabelle's turn. She had so much to say and so much for which to be thankful. She picked up Hope's tiny hand and kissed it, gazing at the toddler in the high chair next to her. Then she looked around at her family, in a softer voice than normal, she began to share.

"It's been an unimaginably difficult and at times a crushing past four years. Some days were so dark, I couldn't imagine surviving one more week. But as I sit here, cradled in love and wrapped in gratitude, I am truly thankful for the journey. Do I wish the road had been easier? I absolutely do. But it was what it had to be to get us all here, in this moment, together, sewed meticulously into each other's lives. And so I am truly thankful for this precious family and friends who are like family, who are all so very dear," Isabelle said.

Turning specifically to Owen, Isabelle continued. "Owen, I'm glad you're here. I don't know if or how you will fit into my future, but I'm truly happy to have you join our family today."

Isabelle paused as she prepared to share something that everyone could sense was incredibly important to her. Even

Zach held the jokes he normally would have thrown out to lighten the mood. "Arnie once told me that in life, we all walk through the fire. We can focus on what we lose or we can focus on what we learn and who walks with us on our journey. And above all we can be thankful. And today, I am truly thankful for all of you," Isabelle concluded. Her family and friends nodded in unison. It was a rugged hike they all knew too well.

Owen reached over and brushed Isabelle's hand. "I've never actually participated in anything like this," Owen said. "I was worried I wouldn't have anything to add that would rise to the occasion and be appropriate." This made everyone laugh a little nervously. *Appropriate?* Isabelle wasn't sure where this was going. "I am thankful for Maui and the goofy-foot surfer I met on Honokawai Beach. I'm thankful I invited her to coffee. And I'm thankful she gave me a second chance when I," he stopped to sigh. "Blew it. But I won't go into that. I'm thankful Harriet is well enough to be home and that she invited me to join you today. And I'm thankful that Isabelle understands what a genuine hero I am," he said joking and then breaking out into laughter. "Too much?"

"You're a dork," Isabelle said, smiling and shaking her head.

Harriet quickly took the floor. "I'm thankful for my family, and to have you all back in the house where my sister Joy and I grew up. I'm thankful that my life was spared in the fire, and for my salvation for when it is my time to go. I'm thankful for my grandchildren, those present and those yet to come. I'm thankful for friends and food and a warm place to lay my head. Instead of feeling like I lost everything, in more important ways, I feel like I have been given everything that matters. I'm thankful to Owen for retrieving a very special book that once belonged to my sister. I'm thankful for every rich blessing afforded me on this earth and in the divine above," Harriet said. And without missing a beat or giving the group a chance to toast she took hands and launched directly into grace.

"Our heavenly Father, we thank you. For bringing us together, to serve and to love. For the food that has been prepared and all the hands which have prepared it. For your grace and love throughout all of our days. We thank you for your gifts, your light and your great redemption, by which we are connected both in this life and the next. We thank you for this very special Thanksgiving together in this home, and we ask that you bless this meal to our bodies. In your blessed name. Amen." As Harriet closed her prayer, Owen squeezed Isabelle's hand, and when she looked up at him, and smiled, she squeezed his back.

It was in that moment that Isabelle noticed the large family photo, hanging on the far wall. *Wow.* She had forgotten that photo existed or she would have requested a copy of it sooner. It was her original family. Grandma and Grandpa Barth, her dad, Jack, her mom, Joy, Frank and Harriet and Zach and her. Zach looked to be about five in the photo which would have made her three. She had no recollection of this photo being taken, but she knew she wanted a copy of it for her own dining room at home.

She recognized that the photo was taken outside the farmhouse in the yard, and this sparked a grand idea. "Hey Alexa, what do you think if we recreate that photo after dinner with everyone who's here today?" Isabelle suggested. "I think your other wall could use a modern day family picture."

"I love that. What a great idea," Olivia spoke up.

"Let's do it!" Alexa said.

After dinner, everyone was happy to move around and be part of a picture that would remind each of them that families come in all shapes and kinds.

It took some maneuvering to fit in the adults, kids and toddlers, and get everyone to smile at the same time, but it was just the day for a Thanksgiving miracle. Oddly enough, no one had a selfie-stick, but fortunately, The Shireys were walking by with their dogs. Alexa called out to Dr. Shirey and his wife. He was more than happy to snap a perfect fall photo of their first Thanksgiving together. None of them would need a picture to remember this special day, but what a grand souvenir it became. A reminder of a week that started with a fire and ended with a warm, safe place for all to call home.

EPILOGUE: THE BRIDGE

Isabelle took a deep breath as she looked around at her amazing family. A genuine and satisfying smile took residence on her face as her joyful eyes watered just enough to appear glassy, but not so much to spill a single tear down her face. Isabelle was all too familiar with this spot – not just the geography, but that tender space filled with both gratitude and loss – the one that kept her equally hopeful and grateful throughout the years. She inhaled deeply, never imagining life would turn out so good.

She looked over at Zach and Amone, proud parents of Jaxson Jacob and Donna Joy. She looked at her little Hope, grown up and a successful young career woman in every sense of the word. *Where did the time go?* She turned her head to Carrie and Richard – and Pinky, who had recently started introducing herself as Penelope Rae. *I guess we all grow up sometime.* She glanced left to Sal and Agus's daughters, Olivia and Alexa, Alexa's husband Doug, and their daughter Judy – who was engaged to her nephew Jaxson, with a wedding planned two days away. She couldn't help but smile, thinking back nearly three decades, to the day she spoke those tender words about Arnie. *It's hard to believe you've been gone nearly thirty years, love? Another celebration of life and another wedding.* She smiled.

She glanced to the right and smiled at Grace. Grace – a most incredible child, who grew up to be an even more incredible woman – now a professor at New York University. "Aunt Liberty took Henry for a walk so he wouldn't do his business in front of everyone on the beach," Grace informed her mom nonchalantly. "She'll be back." Grace still made Isabelle laugh.

As Isabelle looked around, and inhaled joy, she leaned back into the strong and open arms of her husband, Owen, whose secure embrace held her tightly for nearly twenty-five years. Smiling, she turned around and snuggled her head into his broad chest. He smelled so good to her, and he still made her feel unimaginably safe.

"You gonna to be okay?" Owen asked. She nodded affirmatively. "I'm here, and I'm not going anywhere." He had been saying these same words to her for twenty-five years, since that Thanksgiving night, when he first took her hand at dinner, and in exchange, gave her his heart.

While they had gathered for Harriet's celebration of life, Isabelle and Owen shared a secret. Isabelle's cancer had returned, and they decided together not to share it with the family until after the wedding. Over the years, Owen had become the friend, partner, husband, champion and lover for whom Isabelle had always prayed, and hoped would come. Even with family and friends so close, they shared their own world, their own references and their own bond. Maui was their special place. It was here that they first met, later married, and renewed their commitment to each other year after year. And so while they vowed to fight cancer together, yet again, they savored the moment, as they did each day, ensuring every beautiful memory they created together would last a lifetime to whichever of them outlived the other.

Liberty returned with her golden retriever, Henry, just as Isabelle finished gathering her thoughts. As Isabelle reached out to take Grace's hand, Owen released his grip on his wife. But just before stepping toward the ocean to give the eulogy she wrote so many years before, in honor of the woman who had given her everything but life itself, she turned quickly and leaned in to kiss Owen one small peck on the lips.

Isabelle and Grace walked hand-in-hand to the water's edge, holding together a plumeria lei. Isabelle had a speech prepared, with all the usual facts and elements. But as Isabelle looked up, at the perfect white clouds hung against a crystal blue sky, she saw assembled a choir of angels – with familiar faces that nearly took Isabelle's breath away. "Do you see them?" Isabelle whispered to Grace.

"I do, mom. There's Dad and Yia Yia. Sal and Agus. Who are…" Grace started to ask.

"Those are your Grandma Joy and Grandpa Jack, and my Grandma Mae and Grandpa James. Tim. Evelyn. They are all here with us, honey" Isabelle said, smiling in wisdom, as happy tears continuously streamed down her face like the edges of an infinity pool. Everybody she had ever loved surrounded them on shore at the water's edge, and up above in the clouds in spirit.

"Mom, are they real? Are they really here?" Grace whispered.

"Yes darling, they are very real. Those we love live forever in our hearts. They are a part of us and are always with us," Isabelle whispered back.

And that's exactly how Isabelle started the eulogy to Aunt Harriet, who lived more than twenty-eight years past the diagnosis doctors imagined would take her life back when she first suffered the hemorrhagic stroke. It was this stroke that first inspired Isabelle to get to know her aunt as an independent woman, who in her own meddling way, deeply cared about

Zach, Isabelle and the eclectic family they weaved together over the years. Harriet was ninety-six years old when she passed peacefully in her sleep.

"Harriet once confided to me that she was once sad that she and Uncle Frank never had children of their own. This feeling triggered immense guilt when our parents died in the car accident. She received the children she always wanted at the cost of the person she loved most in this world – our mom. Isn't it ironic that the woman who believed she would never have a family of her own is the reason we are all gathered here together today? Whether by blood or by love, we are family. And without Harriet, who knows if Zach and I would have even been raised in the same home, let alone been fortunate enough to be grown up and adopt all of you. If we were a family broken by tragedy, we are equally a family sewn together by love," Isabelle said.

While the eulogy Isabelle gave for Arnie a quarter century before left everyone a bit sad, today was a different story. The poignant lessons she had learned from Harriet and a life well lived, gave Isabelle the perspective to leave the family inspired and hopeful this time around. When she and Grace were finished speaking, everyone cheered as Grace bent down and placed the lei at the edge of the tide.

Isabelle reached up to her own neck and felt the fine strand of variegated pink coral pearls that Harriet had once given to her. She had long thought about which of her daughters to give it to but had come to the conclusion of what Harriet would have wanted. "Judy, darling, could you please come here?" she asked, surprising everyone. She reached up and took off the pricey strand of pearls. "In two days, you will marry my nephew, officially merging two families who have been the dearest of friends for decades. This coral strand belonged to Harriet, the only Yia Yia Jaxson, Donna, Grace and Hope ever knew. I am not lending these to you. These are for you. They are your something-old. Someday, you will be a part of the generation that continues this ever-changing gift of family. It may be a family of blood and it may be a family of love. There will be celebrations and there will be set-backs. But whatever it is, give yourself and your heart to it fully – and all the joys and blessings of a magnificent life will one day surprise you with how truly good life can be." Isabelle embraced Judy, pulling her tight and kissing her cheek.

When the family dispersed back to their condos, Isabelle stood on the shore, gazing to the horizon where the sun had set, hand-in-hand with her great love. Isabelle once loved Arnie – as much as she was capable of at the time. But after she and Owen settled their misunderstandings, on that Thanksgiving evening so many years before, they vowed together to tackle every mountain and valley life presented together.

It was Arnie who had told her to not give up on love, and she always wondered if in some unexplainable way, Arnie hand-picked Owen, right here in the islands, as the man who would love Isabelle in a way even he never could.

Isabelle was determined to fight and beat this latest round of cancer. She was confident it wasn't her time. But when it was, she knew she would be ready. Her faith in God, family, love and the fact that good ultimately conquers evil was strong. Many times she reminded her children and anyone else who would listen of Arnie's loving words, "We all walk through the fire, but what matters more than what we lose, is what we learn and who walks with us on our journey."

ACKNOWLEDGEMENTS

Very special thanks to my development editor and friend, Timothy Jeske, Ph.D. You signed up for one book, and ended up guiding me through three books and four stories – one for each book and an overreaching story that is only discovered by those who journey through all three books. You offered this as a full gift of your time, talent and heart for a friend, at a time I truly had nothing to offer but my gratitude. I couldn't have told this story as succinctly and perfectly stitched without your guidance.

Thank you to Chevy Cortez, who is a talented graphic designer and one of the finest people I know. I met Chevy through non-profit work, where he gifted so much time and talent to our local community. I'm fortunate to include him in this very special finale to my *Gift of Grace* trilogy.

Thank you, Aunt Harriet, for giving me truly awesome insight into my mom. We live in such a polarized world, where so many people can no longer even be friends with people who share a different perspective or opinion. My mom and I will always see the elephant from different angles. Getting to know her through the eyes of Aunt Harriet helps me better understand her through her eyes rather than my lens. Harriet desperately loves Isabelle, even when they disagree. The journey of writing this trilogy has been a reminder how much my mom fully and overwhelmingly loves me, despite our differences and communication acrobatics.

Thank you to my sister, mom, dad, and dear friends who saw me through some really tough years and big life lessons. This trilogy follows Isabelle's struggle through a challenging time, debilitating grief, recovery from loss, and finally, her emergence into the truly magnificent woman she was destined to be.

People have asked me if Isabelle was based on my life, given the fact that Harriet was inspired by my mom. She was not. She encounters trials and achieves victory in the end, as I hope my life will follow. More than anything, this trilogy has given me a greater understanding of and relationship with my mom, while she is still living. It has given me compassion and tolerance for our disparate views, and it has brought us closer. This is the greatest gift for which I could have hoped.

We all walk through the fire. We can focus on what we lose, or we can focus on what we learn and who walks with us on our journey.

ABOUT THE AUTHOR

Debra Yergen started writing as a child. She views story-telling as a vehicle to transcend differences and bridge the values we all hold dear. As a corporate writer, she created case studies that revealed the journey to success. As a fund developer, she shared the success stories that were made possible through gifts large and small, and invited donors to see their contributions as the key to solutions for those in need.

Debra is an award-winning copywriter with six national advertising awards.

Debra received her Bachelors of Arts degree in Broadcast Journalism from the Edward R. Murrow School of Communication at Washington State University. She received her Business Administration certificate from the Michael G. Foster School of Business at the University of Washington.

Debra has authored ten books, including business and economic books, devotionals, a cookbook and her fictional Gift of Grace trilogy. Debra's books have debuted on Amazon's #1 New Release list three times. She has been interviewed by the world's leading media sources. Links to articles are available at www.DebraYergenCo.com

If you enjoyed this book, please follow Debra, and write a review on Amazon.

Find her on Twitter @Debra_Yergen and on Facebook at https://www.facebook.com/AuthorDebraYergen/

BOOKS BY DEBRA

Real Life 101: Winning Secrets You Won't Find in Class

Creating Job Security Through Mobility and Diversity

Creating Job Security Resource Guide (series)

Facing Forward A Life Reclaimed

Sweet Pickles Take Time: 12 Days of God's Love & Grandma's Recipes

Finding My Dazzle: A Zebra's Journey, The Andi Creed Story

The Eulogy

The Bench

The Gathering

Grace Knows Your Name, 30 Days of Thanksgiving

COMING SOON: Social Distancing, An Extrovert's Survival Guide

www.ingramcontent.com/pod-product-compliance
Lightning Source LLC
Chambersburg PA
CBHW031128130726
47988CB00006B/2281